Pouliuli

Albert Wendt

The University Press of Hawaii
Honolulu

Pacific Classics Edition 1980

Library of Congress Cataloging in Publication Data

Wendt, Albert, 1939–
 Pouliuli.

 (Pacific classics ; no. 8)
 I. Title. II. Series.
PZ4.W472Po 1981 [PR9665.9.W46]   823   80–15158
ISBN 0–8248–0728–6

PACIFIC CLASSICS

1. The Return of Lono: A Novel of Captain Cook's Last Voyage   *O. A. Bushnell*
2. My Samoan Chief   *Fay G. Calkins*
3. In the South Seas   *Robert Louis Stevenson*
4. Molokai   *O. A. Bushnell*
5. Mark Twain's Letters from Hawaii   *edited by A. Grove Day*
6. Island Nights' Entertainments   *Robert Louis Stevenson*
7. Ka'a'awa: A Novel about Hawaii in the 1850s   *O. A. Bushnell*
8. Pouliuli   *Albert Wendt*

For Jenny

Chapter 1

Early on a drizzly Saturday morning Faleasa Osovae—the seventy-six-year-old titled head of the Aiga Faleasa, faithful husband of a devoted Felefele, stern but generous father of seven sons and five obedient daughters, and the most respected alii in the village of Malaelua—woke with a strange bitter taste in his mouth to find, as he looked out to the rain and his village, and then at his wife snoring softly beside him in the mosquito net, and the rest of his aiga (about sixty bodies wrapped in sleeping sheets) who filled the spacious fale, that everything and everybody that he was used to and had enjoyed, and that till then had given meaning to his existence, now filled him with an almost unbearable feeling of revulsion—yes, that was the only word for it, revulsion. He despised everything he had been, had become, had achieved: his forty years as a deacon and lay preacher; his almost unlimited power in the matai council; his large profitable cacao plantation; his title as the highest-ranking matai in Malaelua; his nationally respected reputation as an orator; his detailed knowledge of genealogies and history, which was envied by other matai; his utter loyalty and devotion to his village and aiga and church; his unquestioned reputation as a just, honourable, courageous, and humble man of unimpeachable integrity; and his perfect health. (In his seventy-six years he had only been seriously ill once. He still had nearly all his teeth and hair.) Even the familiar smell of his fale and relatives now repelled him. He sniffed back the mucus in his nose, caught it at the back of his throat, pulled up the side of the mosquito net, and spat it out on to the paepae. But the feeling of nausea surged up from the centre of his chest and he started coughing loudly, repeatedly; and then he was vomiting uncontrollably, the thick, half-digested food and bile and stench shooting out of his mouth and over his sleeping wife who, a few offended seconds later, was awake and slapping him on the back and calling to her daughters to bring a basin. But when the first bout of painful spewing stopped, Faleasa pushed her away through the side of the net, which tore with a protesting R-R-RIP-P, and toppled out on to a group of their sleeping grandchildren who woke up screaming and woke the whole aiga, who, in turn, scrambled up and around a now weeping Felefele and a Faleasa who advanced shouting at them to get out of *his* fale and scattered them with his kicking feet and flailing fists. And soon they were all through the fale blinds and over the paepae into neighbouring fale and houses which belonged to their aiga and from which, safe from Faleasa's inexplicable wrath, they observed him fearfully, unwilling to agree with Elefane, the eldest son, that their up-to-then-was-always-sane father was now suffering a spell of insanity or that an aitu had taken possession of him during the night by entering his brain, lungs, heart, and belly, especially his belly, because no human being could spew out that unbreathable amount of vomit.

'What are we to do?' Felefele asked. (All the neighbouring aiga were awake by then; and most of them were on their paepae and verandas enjoying Faleasa's performance.)

'We shall never be able to live down this disgrace,' her daughters said.

Faleasa ripped all the mosquito nets from the strings that tied them to the rafters and hurled them out of the fale—the paepae was shrouded with white netting. He then gathered all the pillows, sleeping sheets, and mats and threw them out as well. Felefele sent some of the girls to bring her treasured possessions out of the rain but, as they approached, Faleasa threatened to kill them if they touched anything, so they retreated to Felefele who, no longer worried about her husband's health but extremely angry with him, stood up arms akimbo and called to him to stop being childish and think about how their village would view his senile behaviour—she emphasised the word senile, which angered Faleasa more and made him grab the large wooden chest in which all their clothes were kept, pull it clattering across the pebble floor to the front paepae, take out armfuls of clothes and scatter them across the paepae and grass, all the time exclaiming loudly that his wife and children and relatives were a pack of greedy, gluttonous, uncouth, uncivilised dogs. When the chest was empty he rolled it down the paepae; it broke into large pieces. He then sat down cross-legged in the middle of the fale, arms folded across his heaving chest, head held high defiantly, the nausea gone. 'Stay like that for all we care!' Felefele called. Then she ordered their aiga not to pay any attention to their *sick* father but to go about their normal activities as if he wasn't there.

He would remain in this position that whole morning, thought Faleasa, as though saying to everyone that he had the inalienable right to defy them and to own nothing but an empty fale, the defiant breath in his lungs, the pools of rapidly drying vomit and their honest stench; and no one, absolutely no one, was going to take any of them away from him. No one dared—the people of Malaelua went about their normal chores; so did his aiga, but they paused often to observe him. At about ten o'clock, the rain having stopped, Felefele sent Elefane to him with a foodmat laden with his favourite food—faalifu talo, home-made cocoa, and fried pisupo. Elefane didn't even reach the edge of the paepae before an unfatherly stone whispered past his head. He wheeled swiftly and scrambled back to Felefele on his aging forty-five-year-old legs, telling everyone that Faleasa was truly possessed and needed the pastor or a fofo to exorcise the aitu. Felefele sent him to fetch Pastor Filemoni. (It wasn't Christian to get a fofo.)

At noon Faleasa saw Filemoni crossing the road and coming towards him; the pastor's white shirt and lavalava gleamed in the light and distracted Faleasa from Filemoni's smother of flab: Filemoni, only in his early thirties, a recent graduate from Malua Theological College, and Felefele's nephew—which was why, through Faleasa's influence, he had been appointed pastor at Malaelua—was fast achieving obese proportions. Up to this critical morning Faleasa had always been tolerant of Filemoni's inadequacies which were many: for instance, he was extremely lazy and didn't bother to compose inspiring sermons; he was arrogant and from the pulpit chastised everyone, except Faleasa, who offended him; he insisted on receiving large monetary donations for his upkeep at the end of every month; he was a shallow thinker who hid his shallowness behind a mask of glibness, bigotry, and pretensions; his breath stank but he didn't know it because he believed his total body odour to be the sweetest perfume the village of Malaelua had ever breathed; his wife and two children were intolerably spoilt, condescending, disrespectful of the faa-Samoa, an embodiment of the worst characteristics of the town where his wife was born the daughter of a government clerk. But now, as Faleasa watched Filemoni waddling self-consciously (knowing every Malaeluan was observing him) up to his fale, the dizzy spell of nausea started turning inside his head again.

Pompous pile of expensive excrement! Faleasa cursed to himself as Filemoni reached the edge of the paepae, paused, and, standing on the tips of his toes, peered into the fale. Filemoni's eyes lit up when he sighted Faleasa and he hurried up the paepae and sat down opposite Faleasa who stared unwaveringly at him.

'How are you?' Filemoni chose the informal approach (after all Faleasa *was* his uncle), his nostrils breathing warily because the whole fale stank of vomit.

'Touch your arse!' Faleasa greeted him.

Ignoring his uncle's profane remark—it was the first time he'd heard Faleasa, whom he respected, swearing—Filemoni prattled on about how unreliable the weather was. 'Touch your arse and smell your own foul stench!' Faleasa enlarged on his first unique greeting. Again the pastor ignored it. Faleasa raised his voice, his eyes wild with what Filemoni thought was madness, and said, 'Touch your arse and smell your own foul stench because you and your stench deserve each other!' This time Filemoni couldn't ignore it: he, Filemoni Matau, was a Servant of God and the son of an alii and therefore had his self-respect, pride, status, and

4

courage to protect. Faleasa was obviously sick, possessed by a vindictive aitu, so Filemoni gazed forgivingly at him, knowing he had to address the aitu directly if he wanted to exorcise it.

'Demon, what are you doing inside this good old man?' Filemoni asked the aitu.

Faleasa nearly laughed when he realised what their diagnosis of his ailment was but he decided to play along. Deepening his voice to make it sound like his mother's who had died years before, he said, 'I am inhabiting my son's body because I want to destroy his goodness.' He saw Filemoni start to tremble.

'You are his mother?' Filemoni asked. Faleasa nodded his head as if he was now mesmerised by the pastor. 'But why?'

'I can't stand his goodness. As you know, he is the most generous, most compassionate, most honest, most Christian person in Malaelua, and when he dies he will go to Heaven for sure!'

'Demon, evil disciple of Satan,' declaimed Filemoni, 'I order you, in the sacred name of Jesus, to leave the body of this good servant!'

Faleasa laughed his mother's laugh as though he was completely mad, and watched Filemoni cringe with fright. 'Touch your holy arse!' his mother, through Faleasa, shouted at Filemoni. 'You've got no power because you're one of the most wicked men in Malaelua, a Pharisee through and through. Only a truly good man can drive me out, and the only good man in Malaelua is my son whose carcass I now inhabit!' Faleasa continued to laugh shrilly, imitating what he thought was a lunatic's laughter. As he laughed he crawled slowly towards Filemoni. He, after trying frantically to control his fear, jumped up and backed away from Faleasa, who bared his teeth and neighed like a horse. When Faleasa splattered a stream of hot vomit on to Filemoni's legs he wheeled and fled down the paepae and across the malae, not daring to look back and completely forgetting that all Malaelua were witnessing his cowardly retreat.

Faleasa wiped his mouth, aware that for some unknown

5

reason he could vomit whenever he chose to, and decided that he was really enjoying himself. After Filemoni's failure he knew they would resort to a pagan cure—a fofo. After all, he, Faleasa Osovae, was their leader and was therefore worth saving at any cost, even if it meant using cures which the Church condemned as downright heretical. Being possessed and deranged had definite advantages: he could, with impunity, scare the excrement out of all his worthless kin and village.

Hunger tugged at his belly so he yelled for some food. Two of his married daughters, Tina and Palaai, both prodigious breeders, gossips, and relentless schemers who were always after him with their cunning ways to confer matai titles on their worthless husbands, came scrambling into the fale with a foodmat laden with food, a kettle of cocoa, and a basin of water. He tried his best to keep on looking possessed, his eyes glazed with madness, his body stiffly frozen in that defiant posture which was beginning to exact a painful toll on his old muscles, back, and backside. Warily, but still trying to smile, his daughters placed the food in front of him and withdrew to sit at the back posts in readiness to serve him. Still gazing fixedly ahead, Faleasa again used his mother's voice. 'Get out, you scheming whores!' he ordered. When they were out of sight he ate eagerly, quickly. The food tasted delicious.

Nothing about his past, he reflected, seemed real, important, vital, necessary—he had shed it all like a useless skin. Yes, he had been reborn; but he realised they would not accept his new self: they needed him to be the thoroughly domesticated, generous, always-willing-to-sacrifice-him-self-for-them father, provider, arbitrator, floormat. They had grown accustomed to the taste of his old carcass. Now they would choke on the poison of his new self. He chuckled at the thought.

He finished eating, washed his hands in the basin of water, and threw everything out on to the paepae, where the plates, Felefele's best ones, smashed on the stones. Getting his ali— he was the only person in Malaelua who still used one—he lay down and was soon fast asleep. He would need all his physical strength if he was to combat them.

When he awoke the smell of vomit was gone, the fale felt clean, and he found he was covered with a fresh sleeping sheet. He jerked up to a sitting position, suspiciously. They had come in and cleaned the fale. Except for the chest he had broken, everything was back in its normal place, arranged, as always, according to Felefele's sanity, as it were. He started to feel trapped, as though Felefele's orderly mind, in which he now realised he had been living for nearly fifty years, was again closing in round him like a smothering womb. He jumped up and shuffled about the fale, placing well-aimed pools of vomit in strategic positions (for instance, over the mattress of the only bed), and rearranging everything according to the chaotic freedom of his rebirth, as it were. He did his best to appear possessed, utterly frightening to his aiga and to Malaelua, while he did the rearranging.

An hour or so later, not that time seemed important to him any more, while he was lying on his back and gazing up into the fale dome, contemplating nothing (he discovered it was extremely healing to contemplate the Void), he heard the sound of brave footsteps coming up the front paepae and into the fale. He didn't bother to look; he knew what the man's profession was. Filemoni, Christ's man, had failed; now they were turning to the Devil. Faleasa felt the man sit down at one of the front posts, felt the man scrutinising him carefully, felt the hesitancy, the tremors of fear, as the man prepared to talk to him. As he felt all this through his pores —he could describe it to himself in no other way—he realised that here was another marvellous quality of his new self. His wrinkled, scarred, thick hide had achieved a new and miraculous sensitivity: he could see with it, feel with it, think with it.

'Go away!' he said, without bothering to look at the fofo. 'I don't need you.'

The man insisted on greeting him formally and then said, 'But you do need this humble person, sir.' From his sound and feel Faleasa gathered that the man would be physically very small, a tight knot of cunning energy about fifty years old; he would be well-skilled in the subtle manipulation of language to trick unwary victims into parting with their possessions such as aitu, money, ietoga, food; his extra-large skull would be covered with a short-cropped bristle of black hair, his nose almost as wide as a pig's snout, his eyes perpetually darting in search of valuables he could take possession of; and his body would be pock-marked with healed sores, the result of malnutrition in childhood.

'Why do I need you?' Faleasa asked, still gazing up into the fale dome.

The fofo coughed politely. 'Your concerned aiga have told this humble man that you are ill, sir, and urgently in need of this humble person's type of cure.'

'I am not possessed by an aitu, if that's what you mean by being ill.' Faleasa sat up and faced the fofo for the first time. 'Do I look possessed to you?' The fofo studied him from under knitted brows; then his eyes darted to the vomit and chaos in the fale. But, before he could use it as proof that Faleasa was possessed, Faleasa told him that he had wrecked the fale when his nagging wife had angered him. 'You know what wives can be like,' he said. 'They can be very cruel.' The man nodded eagerly, encouraging him to talk on, but Faleasa wasn't going to have any of that and he wasn't going to waste any more time with this charlatan, so he got up, with the man observing his every move, reached up to the lowest fale rafter for the tobacco tin in which he kept his money, returned and sat down only a yard or so in front of the man, opened the tin, emptied all his money on to the mat, and with slow deliberateness counted every note and coin. 'Thirty dollars and forty-five cents,' he concluded. Then, carefully wrapping the soiled notes round the coins, he reached out, clutched the man's right hand, turned it palm upwards, gazed mercilessly into his eyes, thumped the money on to his palm, closed the man's rough fingers round it, and said: 'If you think I've got an aitu in my guts then you can return all that money to me. But, if you believe what I've said, that I'm as healthy as you are, then you may keep the money as a contribution from this humble old man to help pay your travelling expenses.' The

8

man bowed his head but made no move to return the money. 'Put it in your shirt pocket,' Faleasa suggested. The man's hand obeyed him. 'Now that our small problem has been solved what shall we discuss?'

'This humble person is a poor man with a large hungry aiga, sir,' the man confessed, his head still bowed.

'Who isn't poor?' interrupted Faleasa.

'That's why this worthless person has accepted your generous gift, sir,' continued the fofo.

'Don't worry,' Faleasa said, 'your honour and self-respect are still intact. There is no need to feel you have sold them to this worthless old man.' The man smiled. 'Don't go yet. I have gifts for your wife and hungry children as well.' Faleasa went over to the ola in which, while he had been asleep, Felefele had stored all their aiga's clothes, selected the best dresses, lavalava, and shirts, and piled them into the fofo's willing lap. 'And you don't need to thank this worthless old man for these things,' he said. 'On your way out go to my aiga who got you to visit me and thank them; the clothes belong to them.' The man nodded, mumbled thank you, thank you, and got up to go. 'Would you do one small favour for this worthless old man?' Faleasa asked.

'Anything,' the fofo replied, 'anything, sir!'

'When you discuss the case of this helpless old man with his strong aiga tell them that you failed to drive the aitu out of this old man's entrails.' The fofo nodded again and hurried out of the fale.

Faleasa watched him enter the fale in which Felefele and her scheming brood were waiting for him. When they saw he was watching they lowered the fale blinds. Faleasa rested his cunning head on his ali and smiled triumphantly.

That evening after he had bathed in the pool he returned home to find that his fale had been tidied and his aiga were gathered in it ready for their evening lotu. He examined them disdainfully, dressed behind a curtain that Felefele had strung across the side of the fale where he slept, then emerged and commanded them to leave him alone. If they dared send him another insane fofo, he said, he would put fatal curses on all of them. Felefele and some of their daughters and grandchildren started to cry, but he ordered them to get out of *his* fale and said that from then on there would be no more lotu—he didn't believe in that Christian nonsense any more. Elefane started to declaim a speech he had prepared to try to placate his father but Faleasa told him to shut his hypocritical gob and get out. Felefele accused him of not loving them any more but he only laughed loudly and maniacally, which frightened the children into a shrieking cacophony of tears, and told them to have their ridiculous lotu somewhere else, this fale was his and only his and nobody was to enter it without his permission. They left and he soon heard them having their lotu in the next fale. He got out the large transistor radio which he had bought on his last visit to Apia to sell some cacao beans and turned it up full volume; the blaring sound of guitar music soon drowned out not only his aiga's lotu but the whole neighbourhood's, and he knew that next day the matai council would meet to discuss his behaviour, especially his humiliation of their pastor. He also knew that no matter how irate the council was with him it wouldn't fine him because its members would still be afraid of his power, and fining a madman possessed by an aitu would make them look ridiculous and very unchristian. They would only caution his aiga to keep him under firm control, and say that if he broke any more bylaws they would impose heavy penalties on his aiga—after all, possessed persons weren't responsible for their irresponsibility. Good! he laughed to himself, good!

Because he had spent seventy-six years living like them, *being* them, he could predict their every move, a great advantage in his exhilarating battle for survival as a free man. For example, their next move would be for Filemoni, Felefele, and Elefane to organise his best friends to visit him and try to talk him out of his aitu (and vice versa). Filemoni would lead the delegation because he suffered from delusions of grandeur; and he would be braver than on his first visit because he would have a gang to back him.

When the lotu were over Faleasa switched off the radio and yelled to his aiga to bring him his evening meal and be quick about it. His food was served on tin plates. He'd *solve* that. He ate hungrily, washed his mouth and hands, and then bent every plate, implement, and cup in half and threw them out on to the paepae. From the kitchen fale he heard Felefele's muffled cursing when the women showed her the damaged implements and utensils. He also heard his quick-tempered youngest son, Moaula, who was in his late thirties and married to a sullen woman, exclaim: 'The ungrateful old fool. I should go and knock the insanity out of his head!' (He wouldn't dare of course because assaulting one's parent was taboo.) Moaula was his favourite son; he possessed much courage, a quality sadly lacking in all his other children. 'Don't ever talk about our father that way again!' Faleasa heard Elefane warn Moaula. Faleasa wondered how long it would take before his beloved aiga started warring among themselves. He would play off one faction against the other—a technique he was master of after years of manipulating Malaelua politics.

After five games of patience it dawned on him that this was the first day in his adult life he hadn't said any prayers, hadn't sung any hymns, hadn't read the Bible, hadn't pretended to like his thirty or so snotty-nosed grandchildren, hadn't made decisions that suited everyone but himself, and hadn't sacrificed a little bit more of himself for the sake of his aiga, village, and church. He whooped piercingly and noticed all his neighbours and aiga gazing in his direction. Some of the elders shook their heads sadly. Alas, such a good man now driven insane by the Devil, he imagined them saying to one another. Fools! he thought.

Moaula's wife, Solimanava, and two of her young daughters entered hesitantly to hang up his mosquito net. He continued listening to the radio and playing patience. They moved round quietly, not daring to attract his attention. He pointed at the centre of the fale and they strung up the net there, spread out his sleeping mats, put his ali at the head of the mats, and crept out of the fale.

'Thank you,' he said to Solimanava in his most un-insane voice. She gasped audibly with relief, her sullen face breaking into a grimace of surprise. 'Thank you,' he repeated, 'but tell your stupid husband to copulate some joy and sense into you!' He bared his teeth at her and she almost screamed as she turned and fled, with his best insane laughter chasing her.

He put out his hurricane lamp, got under his net, stretched out, with his head on his ali, and gazed up into the dark healing Void (so he called it). Later, with the muffled sound of the surf brushing at his ears, he thought about what would happen the next morning, and enjoyed anticipating it: he would destroy Filemoni, who owed his pastorship to him and had proven utterly unsuited to the position, and maybe *save*, yes, that was the word for it, save some of his closest friends, whom Filemoni would bring with him, from the self-destroying ritual. He especially wanted to save Laaumatua Lemigao, his most precious companion since childhood.

It was well into the morning but he remained in his mosquito net. His daughters brought him his morning meal and he ate it inside his net, which further persuaded everyone that he was truly possessed. When his daughters tried to talk to him he behaved as if they were invisible, and they left in tears. He had discovered that silence was another effective weapon he could use against them. So, while he lay in his net, waiting for Filemoni and his cohorts to arrive, he rehearsed how he would use that silence. He injected a look of uncomprehending indifference into his face, his eyes assumed a dead withdrawn look, and a little later he succeeded in manufacturing enough spittle to dribble slowly out of the corners of his mouth. He sat up and practised his new act repeatedly.

This was how Filemoni and three of Faleasa's best friends found him. When Felefele saw the party entering Faleasa's fale she sent a daughter to take down his net. She did so with her father sitting there dribbling, and withdrawn into an infuriating silence, which, when she told Felefele and Elefane about it, they interpreted as the final silence of the possessed, the bedevilled.

Filemoni and his group of persuaders greeted Faleasa formally, according to custom. No reply, no reaction: just the dead eyes, the slow dribble, the almost imperceptible rocking of the body backwards and forwards, the flies buzzing round it.

'He's got worse,' Filemoni whispered to the others. They nodded and continued to stare at Faleasa who noticed that Laaumatua Lemigao wasn't with them.

'What are we going to do?' Sau, who was in his sixties, asked Filemoni. He only shook his head sadly.

'Yes, what are we going to do?' the other old men, Tupo and Vaelupa, asked.

'It's probably his age that's made his mind go,' said Sau. Tupo and Vaelupa agreed with him but Filemoni disagreed strongly.

'No. When I visited this unfortunate but venerable old man yesterday I clearly heard his dead mother speaking through him. There can be no doubt about that. He is possessed by an evil aitu.' For the next fifteen minutes or so they discussed Faleasa's condition without bothering to whisper any more. From this, Faleasa concluded, his act had convinced them that he couldn't comprehend anything.

'But why his mother's aitu?' Filemoni asked. 'His mother loved him.'

'It's probably an aitu pretending to be his mother so we would think twice about exorcising it,' suggested Vaelupa, who, Faleasa remembered, was respected in Malaelua for his logic. Tupo, who was always easily dominated by the other matai but whom Faleasa admired for his warmth and kindness and humility, agreed with Vaelupa but suggested that they shouldn't discuss the matter too loudly as the aitu inside Faleasa might be listening to them.

'Just look at his eyes,' said Sau. 'Does he look as if he's hearing anything?' Faleasa almost blinked, unable to believe the lack of concern in Sau's remark, but he was still hopeful that Sau was his friend—fifty years of believing this was difficult to erase from one's heart. Sau erased it with his next remarks: 'We all know, he's always been slightly odd, arrogant, and too dictatorial—mind you, that doesn't mean I disliked him. But that's why this tragedy has happened to him. One can almost say he is being punished by the Almighty for his past.' For a painful minute Faleasa couldn't believe it: Sau had surely always been a friend whom he had trusted. The agony of betrayal almost shattered his act. He felt the nausea returning, born out of the depths of his pain, but he swallowed it back when a few seconds later he admitted to himself that Sau was pretentious, hypocritical excrement like Filemoni, and he didn't need any of them, not even Laaumatua who hadn't bothered to visit him. He was free. They were still trapped in their excreta and stench. Yes, he was free and could do without the ungrateful wretches he had placed in influential positions in Malaelua.

'Yes, he was always a hypocrite,' said Vaelupa. The fat, elephantiasis-ridden thief! Faleasa cursed to himself, remembering how, when Vaelupa had secretly used Malaelua funds and he had found out before the council did, Vaelupa had pleaded with him and he had paid back all the money himself.

'That's not true!' Tupo said. Sau, Vaelupa, and Filemoni ignored his remark. 'That's not true,' Tupo repeated more loudly. They gazed at him as though saying, So what! you're not important, and Tupo looked dejectedly at the floor. The wretches, like his aiga, had used him all these years. What a naive, gullible person he must have been.

'As another human being in need of our help we must help him,' Filemoni said.

'But how?' Sau asked.

'Perhaps we should take him into the Apia hospital and get one of those clever palagi doctors to examine him,' Tupo said after the others had failed to come up with any useful suggestions. Faleasa agreed with Tupo but he saw the others shake their heads and dismiss the suggestion with clicking tongues.

'He's not ill physically,' said Filemoni.

'Palagi doctors don't know how to cure Samoan illnesses anyway,' Sau added. 'And this is a Samoan illness.'

'He's possessed of an evil aitu,' Vaelupa elaborated further. Tupo only looked dejected again.

At that point Felefele and a group of women brought

them food: chicken, pork, fish, baked taro, and palusami. But no one put any food in front of Faleasa. Filemoni hurried through a short prayer, then they attacked the large piles of food. They ate as though Faleasa was invisible or had assumed the unimportant presence of a fly. Only Tupo glanced at him with concern from time to time.

Faleasa waited until they were halfway through their piles of food, then he started to laugh hysterically (or so they believed), with tears streaming from his eyes and saliva drooling out of his mouth. They looked at him, at first with embarrassment and then with sadistic curiosity. He stopped laughing abruptly. A breathless silence fell as he scrutinised each one of them.

'They have poisoned you!' he hissed. For a moment they didn't understand. 'There's poison in the food you're eating,' he repeated. Filemoni spat out the food and pushed his foodmat away violently, so did Sau and Vaelupa. Tupo, always the last to realise what was happening, looked at the hunk of taro in his left hand, then again at Faleasa. 'Can you feel the pain yet?' Faleasa asked. 'Feel the poison eating into your greedy stomachs and intestines?'

'He's lying,' Felefele said apologetically. 'Please excuse his behaviour; he doesn't know what he's saying.'

'Get out!' Faleasa ordered her. She stormed out to the kitchen fale. Turning again to the three frightened men, Faleasa said, 'You're going to die. The poison will eat your insides away—slowly!' Filemoni gasped; a low uncontrollable whimpering issued from Sau's trembling mouth; Vaelupa gargled with some water and spat on to the paepae; and Tupo asked:

'Why did you do it, Faleasa?'

Shaking his head slowly, Faleasa said, 'They did!' and pointed at the women of his aiga sitting at the back posts. 'And he did!' and pointed at Filemoni, who protested his innocence with an almost shouted 'No! No! No!' 'Go and die in your own fale!' Faleasa ordered them. 'I don't want you to stink out my fale!' When they refused to leave and Filemoni began to preach to him about behaving like a child. Faleasa hurled handfuls of pebbles from the floor at them.

Tupo got up politely, wished Faleasa well, and left, with most of his honour intact in the eyes of the Malaeluans who had been watching the confrontation. Filemoni, now outraged by a madman's attack on his self-importance, shouted to Faleasa (a helpless madman) to shut his arrogant gob (and immediately lost the little respect the Malaeluans had for him), ordered Faleasa's children to keep their 'insane and violent matai away from human beings' (and immediately turned the whole Aiga Faleasa against him— when Moaula was told about Filemoni's insulting remark he threatened to disembowel, distongue, and dislife Filemoni, cousin or no cousin!). Filemoni realised with horror what his big mouth had just said and what it was going to cost him, and immediately apologised to the whole Aiga Faleasa; but Felefele, standing on the paepae of the kitchen fale, ordered him to please leave their fale, and said, they, his loyal cousins and relatives, didn't want to ever see him again. Faleasa, she shouted, was definitely *not* insane! So Filemoni staggered up and stumbled out of the fale, cursing his mouth for getting him into trouble again. Sau and Vaelupa started to apologise to the Aiga Faleasa on behalf of the pastor but Faleasa scooped up more pebbles and scattered them, like stinging spittle, over the two men. They scrambled to their shaking legs and backed out of the fale, vowing to get the council to fine the Aiga Faleasa because of their disrespectful treatment of Pastor Filemoni and them, two high-ranking alii. Faleasa deserved to be possessed and insane, Sau said to Vaelupa when they were a safe distance from Faleasa's fale.

'But why?' Laaumatua asked. Faleasa had just described to his lifelong friend his plan and his transformation from what he called 'cannibal meat' into a 'free angel'. When Faleasa didn't reply Laaumatua exclaimed, 'It's insane!' realised the implications of his remark, and apologised. It was midnight; they had met secretly in the church.

'But you're right, Laau,' Faleasa said, 'it is an insane plan but I'm convinced it's the only *sane* thing I can and must do if I want to remain sane myself.' He paused and then added:

'Perhaps in our insane world in which terror and violence feed on the heart's sinews, what we call insanity or, rather, those people we brand as insane are really the only sane creatures among us. Who knows. For seventy-six years I lived what I now see as an insane existence. I was easy meat for all the cannibals; and the worst, the most rapacious of all, were my own aiga and village.' Alone in the black midnight silence and stillness of the church they were beings without physical form, mere voices trying to hear each other, like spirits who, with the coming of dawn, would disappear from the earth.

'Why did you have to tell me though? Couldn't you have left me alone, safe in my belief that you'd gone mad?'

'I'm not courageous enough to do it alone,' replied Faleasa. 'I need your support, your courage, and your understanding. There are too many cannibals and too few missionaries.' He tried to laugh but couldn't.

'I must go,' said Laaumatua.

Faleasa reached out and held his arm. 'You will help me, Laau?' he asked. Laaumatua tugged his arm away.

They were silent for an awkward space, as the darkness throbbed in their eyes and confined them more tightly in the greater darkness of their individual selves; then Laaumatua said: 'The individual freedom you have discovered and now want to maintain is contrary to the very basis of our way of life. Have you considered that? For over thirty years you, Faleasa, and a few other matai have led our village, and your leadership, as was the ancient practice, has been based firmly on the principle that you exist to serve others, to serve the very people you are now branding as cannibals. A good leader doesn't live for himself but for his people And you, Faleasa, wanted the leadership.'

Faleasa agreed but added: 'If I had my life to live again I would not become a leader. And now all I want for the remaining years of my life is to be free.... Surely I have earned that?' he pleaded.

That week an exciting tale of the ignominious defeat of three sane matai and a pastor by a possessed old man circulated through Malaelua and spilt over into the neighbouring villages. The tale, like any other, grew in complexity, size, and inventiveness as it spread from imagination to imagination, but one basic theme consolidated itself: the old man was the hero, the sane matai and pastor were the villains. Only Laaumatua, who had refused to accompany Filemoni and his party to Faleasa's fale and whom Faleasa had got to start circulating the tale, knew who had coined it.

Chapter 2

Faleasa Osovae and Laaumatua Lemigao were born a week apart but the circumstances surrounding their births were markedly different.

Faleasa, christened Osovae, and with thirty-six years to live before the highest title in the Aiga Faleasa was conferred upon him, was born a healthy screaming child at night in the middle of a violent but short-lived thunderstorm, which the elders of his aiga interpreted as a most favourable omen for his future. He would, they maintained, be as strong and as violently courageous as thunder. He was also born the only legitimate son of Faleasa Vaatele—who had three illegitimate sons by other women—the most ruthless, powerful, and insatiably ambitious matai in Malaelua, and himself the son of Vaipaia, a quietly-suffering, old-before-her-time woman whose only distinction lay in having produced five physically perfect children, four daughters and a son. Finally, as the only son, Osovae was heir to an important alii title, to the largest and most prosperously powerful aiga in Malaelua, to the biggest share of Malaelua land, and to his father's unblemished record as the supreme power in Malaelua.

Laaumatua, on the other hand, was born the illegitimate son of Talanoa, a wayward and ugly daughter of the Aiga Laaumatua, which was the poorest aiga in Malaelua: he and the rest of Malaelua would never know who his father was— Talanoa didn't know either, as it could have been any one of four (or had it been five?) men. Instead of being born a healthy screaming child and during a thunderstorm, Laaumatua whimpered club-footedly into the glaring, painful light of midday and the anger of his disgraced aiga, who immediately branded him with the name Lemigao—Without Manners. Finally, as the only illegitimate and therefore unwelcome grandson of frantically pretentious grandparents, he was not heir to anything, especially to the aiga title Laaumatua which forty years later his friend Faleasa Osovae, who had made himself the most powerful man in Malaelua, manoeuvred the Aiga Laaumatua into conferring on him.

'Hey, Crooked-leg!' Osovae called, but the boy with the club-foot continued to hobble past, head bowed, eyes fixed to the ground, as if he hadn't heard. 'Hey, Crooked-leg, I'm calling you!' Osovae repeated, stepping forward and blocking Crooked-leg's path with his extended arm.

Crooked-leg merely glanced at Osovae's arm, then looked up at him with unflinching disdain and said, 'What do you want?' stepping back as he spoke, and obviously preparing to fight. Osovae hesitated. He had thought Crooked-leg wouldn't dare confront him. 'What do you want?' Crooked-leg repeated, raising his fists.

This certainly wasn't the reaction Osovae had expected, so he shook his head, lowered his arm, and asked, 'What's your name?'

'None of your business,' replied Crooked-leg, starting to walk away.

Osovae let him go a few paces. Then he called, 'Hey, Crooked-leg, your leg's falling off!' After what happened next Osovae never again believed that Crooked-leg couldn't move as swiftly as other boys. BANG! Pain exploded in his head and his ears rang as he toppled to his knees. Then more fists jabbed at his head and he was on his back and crying.

'Don't ever call me that again!' Crooked-leg threatened him. Osovae tried to get up but Crooked-leg pinned him to the ground with his knees. 'I'll make you eat dirt again if you ever do!'

Blinking away his tears, Osovae looked up. Crooked-leg's fists were poised directly above his face, ready to shoot down, so Osovae shut his eyes again, turned his face away, and said, 'I won't do it again.'

Crooked-leg jumped to his feet, reached down, grabbed

Osovae's hand, and pulled him up. As Osovae stood drying his eyes with the end of his lavalava, Crooked-leg brushed the dirt off his back and shoulders. 'You shouldn't be rude to people like that,' he kept saying. Ashamed of his defeat, Osovae started to walk away but Crooked-leg blocked his path, smiled, and extended his hand. Head still bowed, Osovae shook hands. 'Your name's Osovae, eh?' Crooked-leg asked. Osovae nodded. 'Lemigao—that's my name, Crooked-leg added. 'You want to come with me?' Without hesitation, Osovae nodded. Lemigao—and Osovae never again called him Crooked-leg (not to his face anyway)— smiled, wound an arm round Osovae's shoulders, and in silence they walked through the village. Osovae didn't know where Lemigao was leading him and he didn't care: all he cared about was that Lemigao was his new friend, his best friend, whom he trusted utterly.

Lemigao was always hungry, or so it seemed to Osovae. Everywhere they went Lemigao searched for food before he did anything else. Inevitably, on their many fishing, shrimping, and bird-hunting expeditions Lemigao cooked a hearty meal or ate raw fish. Even when they collected coconuts in the plantations Lemigao, without fail, ate the first nut he found. He never refused any offer of food even if he had just eaten a large meal. He needed to eat a lot, he was fond of telling Osovae, to be able to carry his 'burden' (as he called his club-foot) around with him. But even though food was the compulsive core of his life he didn't grow fat; his squat frame, pockmarked with countless sores, remained heavily muscled but spare. And, even with his burden, he would brag to Osovae, he could outrun, out-swim, outfish, outfight, outwork, and outeverything all the boys in Malaelua. Not that he had much to do with the other children—he confined his friendship to Osovae, and even to him, in moments of anger, which were rare, as Lemigao hardly ever lost control of his emotions, he would swear he didn't need his friendship. 'I don't need anybody!' he once shouted at Osovae. 'And nobody needs you!' Osovae shouted right back. Lemigao immediately broke into uncontrollable sobbing and beat at his burden with clenched fists. Osovae apologised at once, but Lemigao kept on beating at his foot, shattering the silence of the plantation with his loud sobbing. Afterwards Lemigao punished Osovae by declaring he wouldn't see him for a week. After the week's ostracism their friendship resumed as if nothing had happened.

When they were fourteen years old it was Lemigao's insatiable appetite that first landed them in serious trouble.

They were on their way to Osovae's aiga's plantation one Saturday morning to get some foodstuffs for their Sunday umu when the pig crossed their path. Before Osovae could stop Lemigao the lethal stone shot out of his expert hand and the pig was on its side, its feet kicking feebly at the desperate air, blood trickling from the deep dent in its forehead where Lemigao's stone had landed.

'What are we going to do now?' Lemigao asked, kneeling down beside the pig and jabbing his fingers into its fleshy flanks.

'Hide it!' replied a frightened Osovae. 'Why did you have to kill it?'

'God is my witness,' said Lemigao, 'I didn't mean to. Being a cripple I'm not good at throwing stones.' Paused. 'Wonder whose pig it is? It's well-fed, isn't it? Just look at all this meat!'

Sensing that his friend's appetite was as usual getting the better of him, Osovae said, 'No, we're not going to eat it. If someone finds out we'll be in serious trouble.'

Lemigao looked up. 'But who's going to find out?' he asked. Osovae looked up and down the track. No one in sight yet. 'Well, who's going to find out?' repeated Lemigao, massaging the animal's ribs. 'It'll be a sad waste if we don't make use of it. After all I didn't mean to kill it.'

Osovae couldn't control himself any longer: he quickly retreated into the trees and urinated. He could hear Lemigao's suppressed laughter. 'Crooked-leg!' he cursed his friend under his breath. When he returned he found to his dismay that Lemigao had put the pig in one of the large coconut-frond baskets they had brought with them and thrust his wooden yoke through the top of the basket. Before Osovae could protest Lemigao asked him to help carry the pig to the plantation. Osovae refused. Lemigao immediately said that they were in trouble already for killing the pig so why not make use of the meat. Osovae refused again. 'All right,' shrugged Lemigao, 'I'll leave it here. Someone will find it, and we'll still be in trouble.' He started to roll the pig out of the basket. Osovae grabbed the front of the yoke and lifted his end of their load. Lemigao smiled as he lifted up his end, and said how good the pork would taste when it had been cooked in an umu. They carried the pig to the middle of Osovae's aiga's plantation. They couldn't take it to his aiga's plantation, explained Lemigao, because his relatives were there planting crops. Osovae had to believe him.

They cooked and ate most of the pig.

On the Monday evening, after their lotu, Osovae's father told everyone that there was to be a tautoga for males of all ages the next morning. Stealing, especially pig stealing, was on the increase and the matai council wanted to put a stop to it.

It was as though fear was something Osovae had never experienced before, a force devastatingly new and unbearable, stabbing through his every pore. He escaped into the darkness behind their fale, squatted down, and, while he defecated uncontrollably, cried softly. 'Crooked-leg! Crooked-leg!' he cursed Lemigao, as he cried up into the few stars blinking in the sky's black hide. Crooked-leg was to blame for it all; so it was Crooked-leg's responsibility to get them out of it!

'Why does your father want to go and do that?' asked Lemigao, when Osovae told him about the tautoga. 'Why does he want to try to ruin everything?'

'You'd better think of something to get us out of this,' Osovae cautioned him.

'You ate a lot of the pork too!'

'But you killed the pig!' Because Lemigao was not crying, Osovae was determined not to either.

'I don't want to argue,' said Lemigao. 'Let's just sit quietly and try and think of something sensible to do.'

As they sat silently in the darkness Osovae started to feel less afraid; he always felt more confident when Lemigao was around because he seemed in control of any situation; his burden seemed to anchor him securely to the earth. From where they sat they could see in the main fale, clearly outlined in the light of a hurricane lamp, Lemigao's aiga having their evening meal. But this familiar sight and its warm sound failed to console them.

'Should we just confess everything?' Osovae suggested.

'But how can we do even that?' said Lemigao. Osovae didn't answer, and Lemigao added, 'You could tell your father tonight, then he won't go through with the tautoga?'

'No!' Osovae almost shouted.

'But why not?' insisted Lemigao.

So Osovae had to confess it finally: 'I'm very afraid of him. He'd kill me.' Paused. And then, to excuse his fear of his father, added: 'My aiga will also suffer from the disgrace.'

'So you're saying we should keep it hidden?' Lemigao said.

'No, but . . .'

'But what?'

'We can't go to the tautoga and lie our way through it.'

'Why not?' asked Lemigao. Osovae was too afraid to say it. 'Well, why not?' repeated Lemigao.

'If we lie on the Holy Book something bad will happen to us. God will punish us.' Osovae stopped there; he didn't have the courage to explain what holy punishment would befall them.

'You mean we may go blind or drop dead or go nuts?' Lemigao said. Osovae acted as if he hadn't heard. 'All right, so we're back where we started—*nowhere*!' said Lemigao. 'If I had a father, especially a father like yours, who was Malaelua's leading alii, I'd go to him and confess everything, and my father—like all good fathers who love and protect their children—would save us from our village's wrath.'

'You don't know what my father's like,' Osovae said.

'He'll never forgive me. He won't protect us.'

'Doesn't he love you?'

'I don't know,' mumbled Osovae, and this admission suddenly made him feel less afraid of his own fear of what might happen to them. 'I don't know,' he repeated more firmly.

'Do you think God really loves us?' Lemigao asked.

'Everyone says He does.' replied Osovae.

'But we don't really know, do we?'

'No.'

Then Lemigao's challenge came out of the darkness, clearly, boldly: 'Why don't we try and find out?'

'How?'

'By going to the tautoga and swearing on God's Holy Book that we didn't steal that pig. If God really loves us He won't punish us; He'll forgive us.'

After a sleepless night, early in the morning, before the people started arriving for the tautoga, Osovae went and told Lemigao he couldn't go through with it, not with his father administering the oath; but Lemigao reasoned again that God loved them and would forgive them. 'But my father will know I'm lying just by looking at me,' insisted Osovae.

'Just leave it to me,' Lemigao said. 'I'll get us out of it.'

Instead of returning home Osovae had his morning meal with Lemigao and his grandparents. He only picked at his food; his stomach was a hive of agitated hornets; his nerves were guitar strings too tightly tuned. So Lemigao ate both shares of faalifu talo and cocoa in a ravenous bout, as though he didn't have a care in the universe.

After washing the dishes they strolled to Osovae's fale where the tautoga was to be held. On the way Lemigao had to keep reassuring his trembling companion. 'Just leave it to me,' he said every few yards.

The matai occupied all the posts of the fale. Outside, on the paepae and in the shade of the bread-fruit trees, were all the males of Malaelua. Pig stealing was considered beyond the sinful capabilities of females so they weren't compelled

25

to attend this tautoga. Osovae and Lemigao joined a group of their friends who were entering the fale in pairs and going through the tautoga, the youngest first, as was the practice. No one spoke. Osovae started to feel dizzy, nauseated, but he was strengthened whenever Lemigao smiled at him. Osovae's father and another matai deacon sat in the middle of the fale, administering the oath.

Osovae refused to go in but Lemigao held his arm and tugged at him. As they entered, their heads bowed as was the custom, Osovae noticed that Lemigao was walking with a more pronounced limp, rocking like a boat in rough seas. Some of the matai chuckled at the sight of him: most Malaeluans did whenever they saw his club-foot.

'Do they need to?' a matai called to Osovae's father. 'Both of them haven't got hairs yet, and one's badly in need of a new leg!'

'With a burden like that he hasn't got a hope of catching a pig!' remarked another matai. Most of the matai, even Osovae's father, were laughing by then.

Osovae and Lemigao sat down in front of Osovae's father and the other deacon. Osovae couldn't look at his father— the hornets inside him were threatening to burst out of his belly and he swallowed constantly to hold them down. He noticed that Lemigao was gently massaging his club-foot with both hands and that this action had attracted the two deacons' attention to his burden.

'Lemigao doesn't need to,' Osovae's father said to the council, 'but my son will take the oath.' Osovae's fear nearly shot out of his mouth in a gasp but Lemigao saved him again.

'Sir, this person wants to take it too, please,' Lemigao said. Most of the matai laughed. 'If you think, sir, that this *cripple* is not worthy of the tautoga, then he will obey your will,' Lemigao said, his head bowed as if he was on the verge of tears. Osovae's father stopped laughing at once; so did the other matai.

Osovae's father instructed Osovae and Lemigao to place their right hands on the Bible and repeat after him: 'I swear on this most Holy Book that I have not stolen any of my

26

neighbours' property. If I am lying may our Almighty God strike me dead or punish me in whatever manner He considers fit.... '

A safe distance from the crowd round the fale Lemigao burst out laughing. 'See, I told you!' he said. 'God is a God of love!' He hopped a few paces forward on his good foot and then did a cartwheel. He turned and faced Osovae. 'Hey, why are you crying?' he asked. Osovae turned and fled towards the beach. 'All people tell lies sometimes!' Lemigao called; but his friend kept on running as fast as he could, as if he was trying to break free of an invisible and terrifying parasite that had wrapped itself round him.

Osovae fell ill that night and was ill for nearly two weeks; he suffered from high temperatures, bouts of weeping, and stabbing stomach pains. A frightening nightmare of free-falling into a bottomless chasm shattered his sleep nightly and he lost his appetite—the little food he managed to eat he vomited a short time later. The two best healers in Malaelua tried to cure him but they failed, and his aiga, apart from his father, concluded that his illness had been caused by supernatural agents. His father said nothing to this; neither did he stop his aiga from getting a well-known fofo from the next village to treat his son. Osovae did not respond to the fofo's remedies of herbs, incantations, reading of the cards, massage, and poetical exhortations to the 'evil spirit inside this unfortunate boy to come out'. He grew steadily thinner and withdrew into a silence from which he refused to emerge. But at night he talked in his sleep about God and his parents having forsaken him. When Lemigao visited him Osovae didn't recognise him most of the time, and when he did he burst into loud tears.

'You lied at the tautoga, didn't you?' his father asked one day. They were alone in the fale, his father having sent everyone else out. Osovae didn't reply. The pain of his father's fierce slap which exploded at the side of his face he interpreted as forgiveness. So he nodded his head, his eyes brimming with tears. 'Say it!' his father ordered.

'Yes,' he said, 'yes, I lied.' He looked at his father but

saw no forgiveness, only offence that a son of his had lied. This was confirmed when his father almost shouted:

'No true son of mine ever lies. No son born out of my flesh ever lies before God and our village. You have disgraced me! Why did you do it? Haven't I done everything in my power to make you a god-fearing boy? Why did you lie? Answer me!' By this time his father was shouting. Turning his face away, Osovae refused to reply. 'If you weren't sick I would beat it out of you!' Osovae maintained his rebellious silence. 'It was that cripple, wasn't it? He told you to lie!' When Osovae still remained silent his father said, 'I forbid you to ever see him again. Hear me, I forbid you!'

'Lemigao had nothing to do with it,' Osovae said. 'And he's *not* a cripple!' His father raised his arm to strike him. Osovae gazed defiantly at him. His father stood up and stamped out of the fale.

Chapter 3

Just before evening lotu Faleasa saw Moaula arriving from
the plantation with a heavy load of taro. (He had always
been amazed by his son's physical strength.) The usual
evening chorus of cicadas pulsated in Faleasa's ears. He
was feeling fresh as he had just returned from the pool where
he had bathed alone—most Malaeluans were now afraid of
him.

Moaula dumped his load beside the kitchen fale where
Solimanava and their oldest children were helping Felefele
cook the evening meal. And, looking bigger still in the
falling gloom, he stretched his arms and back and looked
over at his father. Faleasa decided that it was time to
inaugurate the second phase of his plan. He waved to
Moaula to come over to him. Moaula hesitated, then,
obviously pretending he wasn't afraid, came into the fale
and sat down at a safe distance from Faleasa.

'How . . . how are you?' Moaula asked.

Faleasa nodded and said, 'I am well.' Moaula looked
amazed. 'I am not insane,' Faleasa declared. 'I never was.
I .was only pretending. Do you believe me?' Moaula
blinked and tried to say something. 'Do you?' Moaula
nodded. 'Good,' Faleasa said. 'Now listen very carefully to
me.' Paused, coughed, and Moaula edged closer to him.
'Your mother and brother are plotting against me. They
want Elefane to have my title now.' Paused. Moaula shook
his head in disbelief. So Faleasa said, 'Look at me carefully.
Do I look insane to you now?' He reached over and, holding
his son's shoulder, asked, 'Do I?' Moaula shook his head.
'You and your wife are the only members of our aiga I
trust totally,' Faleasa declared. 'Your mother and brother
are plotting against *us*. Do you believe me?'

'I'll fix them!' replied Moaula.

'I'm gratified you believe me,' Faleasa said. 'I need you in my fight to stop your unscrupulous mother—who doesn't deserve to be anyone's mother—and your heartless brother —who doesn't deserve to be any human being's brother— from usurping the leadership of our beloved aiga.' He bowed his head and pretended he was almost weeping.

'I'll fix them!' Moaula said again, rising to his feet. 'I'll fix them!'

Faleasa reached out and tugged him down again. 'No, violence won't solve anything. There is a better way. We'll just observe them, wait them out. I'll continue to pretend I'm insane, you continue to pretend I'm insane, and we'll watch them closely. Tell Solimanava our plan but no one else. When I give you the signal we'll move against them. All right?'

Moaula nodded. 'But if they ever hurt you I'll fix them!' Faleasa's admiration of his son's youth and physical strength deepened as he observed Moaula's huge body rippling with anger.

'Starting tomorrow evening, you are all again to have the evening meal with me,' he instructed. 'Insist on it to Felefele and Elefane.'

'What about lotu?' Moaula asked.

'We'll leave that for a while yet.'

As Moaula left he looked back and smiled.

It was a pity Moaula was raw courage without much control or brains, Faleasa thought.

Again pretending he was utterly contained within himself Faleasa ate and watched them. As he had instructed they were all there, about sixty of them, from Felefele and their daughters and daughters-in-law (all large matrons) who were sitting behind the baskets of food, to the youngest child, Moaula's son, who was fast asleep in his father's lap. No one else was eating. No one spoke; even the children, who were by then all afraid of him, tried to keep still. Everyone tried not to look at him but Faleasa occasionally caught some of the adults glancing at him with concern.

When Moaula did so Faleasa winked at him.

He pushed his foodmat away. Immediately all the women scrambled up to bring him the basin of water and the hand towel. He glared and then pointed at Solimanava, who—head held up proudly—brought them. He thanked her with a curt nod, and a wink which none of the others saw. When he finished drying his hands there was another scramble to retrieve the basin and towel. He glared at everyone again and pointed at one of Solimanava's daughters. He felt a weight of angry envy descend on the others, especially on Elefane and his wife, Povave.

As the others ate, Faleasa leant against the post and picked at his teeth with a bit of palm frond.

'Is there anything else you need?' Felefele called to him through a mouth bulging with taro.

'Yes, is there anything else you need?' echoed Elefane. Faleasa kept on picking at his teeth.

Half way through their silent meal Faleasa decided to move again. 'Radio!' he called to no one in particular. He heard the feet of many children pattering across the pebble floor towards the tallboy where the radio was kept. 'Stop!' he ordered. A frightened silence. He looked at the children. Not one of them was bold enough to look at him. He pointed at Moaula's eight-year-old son, who smiled victoriously, marched over, brought the transistor radio, and placed it in front of him. Faleasa waved him away and switched on the radio. He deliberately didn't find the local station but turned up the volume and let the radio buzz and crackle as he tapped his hand on his knee to an imaginary tune.

As he had expected, Felefele was oblivious of everything but the huge helpings of food on her foodmat. Ever since she had stopped having children and he had lost most of his interest in sex—not that such interest didn't still flare up occasionally with the proper inducement—she had become a glutton for food. Now, as he observed her attacking her food, he remembered the times when she had attacked him with her hands and mouth and body and winking clutching womanhood, and he felt roused.

He got up and, while they all watched him, went over and lay down on his sleeping mats. Someone came and switched off the radio.

'Are you sure you don't need anything else?' Felefele called, sucking loudly at some fish bones.

'He seems to be getting better,' said Moaula.

'Yes, he ate a lot tonight,' echoed Solimanava.

'He's worse, definitely worse,' was Felefele's diagnosis. 'I think we'd better take him into Apia to see a papalagi doctor.'

'I agree,' said Elefane.

'But you know how Faleasa feels about papalagi,' objected Moaula.

'I don't care what our father feels about papalagi, only a papalagi doctor can heal him now,' said Elefane.

'And if he doesn't want to go?' Moaula asked.

'We'll force him to go!' replied Elefane.

'No one is going to do anything of the sort to *my* father!' threatened Moaula, and Faleasa wanted to applaud him.

'That's enough!' Felefele stopped the exhilarating quarrel from developing. 'If he isn't better by this week-end we'll take him into Apia.' Moaula got up and stamped out of the fale.

After four such evening meals Elefane and Povave and Moaula and Solimanava were not speaking to each other. They communicated when they had to through Felefele who, by then painfully aware of the widening rift between her sons but unable to heal it, was in a 'frantic nervous condition' (Faleasa's description). The children of the two factions started arguing with one another at every opportunity; the rest of their aiga, as the positions of the two main factions hardened, started choosing sides, thus leaving only Felefele to arbitrate.

The next Sunday evening, after the adults had eaten, the first open confrontation between the leaders of the rival factions took place. The tide was in, and Faleasa inhaled the strong smell of decaying coral in the light breeze, as he lay on his stomach, his head resting on his hands, staring at the mats in front of him, but in fact observing everyone from the corners of his eyes.

It was evident to him that Felefele regretted having suggested that he should see a papalagi doctor. All through the meal she had steered discussion away from that topic. Moaula and Solimanava, young and brasher and more daring, were sitting a few yards to Felefele's left; to her right were their older, less daring but more cunning opponents, Elefane, who was sweating freely, and Povave. Solimanava was picking at a sore on the heel of her left foot, and Povave was picking surreptitiously at her wide nostrils and wiping the dry snot on a corner of her lavalava, while their husbands stared out into the darkness and Felefele tried and failed to light a cheroot. People looked ridiculously stupid when they tried to look courageous, Faleasa thought. If only they could see themselves. But they never would; all was vanity and masturbation. So he might as well spark off the fire that they obviously wanted lit. 'Palagi, palagi, palagi!' he chanted as he continued to gaze into the mats. For a solid moment everyone froze and looked at him. Then, as he had expected, Moaula rushed into the fray.

'My father's not going to Apia to see that palagi doctor!' he declared.

'He shouldn't be made to!' added Solimanava, closing ranks.

Elefane turned on her first. 'Women, especially the ones who married into our aiga, do not speak, let alone decide anything in this aiga!'

Povave maintained a loud silence to prove her husband's point.

'Let us discuss this sensibly,' said Felefele.

Moaula ignored her. 'Why do you *really* want him to be examined by a papalagi doctor?' It was more an accusation than a question.

'What's that supposed to mean?' said Elefane.

'You know what I mean,' Moaula replied angrily.

'There's no need to quarrel!' Felefele interjected. Both men ignored her as they glared at each other, with their wives poised behind them.

'Come out with it!' Elefane demanded.

'You want him declared insane, don't you?' Moaula said.

33

'He *is* insane,' said Elefane. 'All I want is for someone to make him well again.'

Moaula shook his head. Solimanava shook her head too.

'Your brother is speaking the truth,' Felefele said to Moaula.

'No, he's not!' snapped Moaula. 'And my father is *not* insane!'

'He's sick and needs help from a doctor,' insisted Felefele.

'I'm—not—lying!' said Elefane.

'All you both want is for a doctor to declare him insane so Elefane can take over the title,' said Moaula.

A threatening silence crouched round them, as Elefane, Felefele, and Povave struggled to believe they had actually heard what they had heard. Felefele was the first to shatter the silence; she began weeping loudly. 'How can you accuse me of such an evil thing?' she kept repeating.

'Yes, how—how can you?' exclaimed Elefane. 'I'm your brother. I'm his son!' He pointed at Faleasa, who was staring at the mats. 'I...I love him. I love you too!'

'We love him!' cried Povave. 'How can you accuse us of such a sin?' She began weeping too and beating at her knees with clenched fists.

Elefane jumped to his feet and, pointing in the direction of the main road, shouted, 'Get out! Get out now. You don't deserve to be a brother or a son to anyone!'

'You get out!' replied Moaula, rising slowly to his feet. 'You're planning to betray your own father, your own flesh and blood. You have no place in this aiga!' The rest of their aiga and many of their neighbours were now gathered on the paepae, ready to stop them from assaulting each other.

'You have no right to speak to me that way—I'm your older brother!' Elefane shouted, his arms akimbo.

'From this day on I renounce you as my brother,' Moaula answered. 'All you and the heartless woman who calls herself our mother want is my beloved father's title. You want that title so badly you're even willing to expose our father to the scrutiny of papalagi, creatures he despises.' Moaula took two steps towards Elefane who took one step backwards to stand beside Povave. 'You get out of this aiga now!'

'Yes!' threatened Solimanava, rehitching her lavalava as she moved towards Povave.

Felefele's weeping changed to high-pitched wailing. 'No! Brothers must never fight!' she cried.

'All right, if it's a fight you want I'll give it to you!' challenged Elefane, taking another step backwards and further away from Moaula.

'Enough!' shouted Faleasa. They all looked at him. Even Felefele forgot to continue crying. He sat up and—no longer pretending he was insane—said: 'I don't want to be examined by any palagi doctor.' They all sat down and the crowd outside started to disperse. Before his family could speak Faleasa said, 'Summon a meeting of our whole aiga for tomorrow afternoon. I have something important to say to all of you.'

Paused. And, after out-staring Elefane and Moaula (who smiled at him), he ordered them to leave his fale.

They left quickly. Felefele tried to stay but he pointed to the kitchen fale and she left, whimpering and sniffing.

Before the others were awake the next morning Faleasa got Moaula to drag one of their canoes down to the sea, and he went fishing for bonito. At midday he returned home. He had caught only a few fish but he had enjoyed the sea's vast silence. He had something to eat, slept, and woke in the early afternoon to find that most of the elders of his aiga and all other Malaeluans connected to the Faleasa title had assembled in his fale.

After greeting them formally he said, 'I have been very ill. I am sure my illness will recur and I haven't long to live. It is impossible, and undesirable, for me to continue as the head of this aiga—I am too old and too sick. Someone else, someone younger and healthier, has to assume the leadership. All I want for the remaining years of my life is peace and quiet to prepare for my final journey to God.' Felefele and his daughters were weeping quietly by the end of his speech.

Before any of the elders could reply he remembered, and said, 'While I was ill the spirit who inhabited me—yes, it was a spirit—advised me to relinquish all my worldly responsibilities. Do you realise who that spirit was?' he asked rhetorically. Paused. 'My mother. And she claims that my illness is more or less permanent and I am to die soon.' Felefele's weeping immediately grew louder. Faleasa silenced her by saying, 'There is no reason to weep; I have lived a long, happy, rewarding life and it is time for it all to end.'

His oldest cousin, only a few years his junior but a wreck of shrivelled flesh, cataract-infested eyes, shaking hands, and quavering voice—all caused not only by old age but by God as payment for his life of sin (he had been a notorious seducer of women and a cattle and pig thief, and he had been in prison innumerable times)—declared that Faleasa, their beloved alii, must serve as the head of their aiga until the day he died; God and their whole aiga wanted him to do so. Most of the elders reiterated this sentiment. Faleasa counter-attacked by asking, again rhetorically, 'Do you want a madman, and a senile one at that, to be your alii? No!' he answered his own question—the others having signified neither agreement nor disagreement. 'My madness,' he emphasised, 'is a recurring curse; already our beloved aiga is the laughing-stock of Malaelua because of me, so there is only one sane thing to do—you must choose a replacement for me.' The women's weeping nagged at him; he ordered them to go and prepare a meal.

'Who do you want?' he asked. After an appropriately polite silence, during which he further intimidated the elders by out-staring each one in turn, he said, 'My successor must be sane, young, hardworking, honest, absolutely fearless, godly, and utterly devoted to the welfare of our aiga.' Paused. And then added, 'He must be a man who has served our aiga well. Loyal service is the true way to leadership.' They all nodded. He noticed that Elefane, who was sitting with the most important elders although he still had no matai title, was exuding confidence. Vain, brainless fool! Faleasa thought. He looked round for Moaula and found him with the least important members of the aiga at the back posts.

'What about Elefane?' some of the most influential elders suggested. Faleasa pondered quickly and decided it wouldn't be wise to lose their support, not yet anyway, so he said, 'You have a week to think about a successor. We'll meet again and decide then.' The other elders agreed. Elefane looked disappointed.

The following afternoon Faleasa visited his cousin. He was alone, so Faleasa came straight to the point. 'Elefane is not a suitable successor. He is too vain and lazy and, worst of all, he doesn't have the courage and drive needed to lead our large aiga and keep it the most powerful one in Malaelua.'

Finally his cousin managed to ask, 'Who then?' Faleasa told him, explained the reasons for his choice, and, before his cousin could speak, congratulated him on agreeing with his choice. He then said that before the next meeting it would be his cousin's fortunate task to visit all the other elders and persuade them to support *his* choice of successor. 'But our candidate,' his cousin managed to object before Faleasa left, 'is too young.'

'How is your son in New Zealand?' Faleasa asked. (Faleasa had paid the young man's fare to New Zealand eight years before.) 'And how are your two nieces doing as nurses at the Apia hospital?' (Faleasa had paid for the girls high school education.) 'And is your stomach troubling you any more?' (Two years before his cousin had undergone expensive medical treatment for a stomach ulcer, and Faleasa had paid for it.)

His cousin gave his agreement a few minutes later and Faleasa left. Everyone in his aiga owed him debts in one form or another and he was now recalling them to achieve his aims. I am truly my ruthless father's son, he chuckled to himself.

At their next meeting Faleasa got his cousin to speak first. In a long, barely intelligible speech, riddled with homilies and platitudes and annoying ah-ahs, his cousin argued that there was no other choice but Moaula. Felefele and Elefane looked stunned but before they could voice their bitterness Faleasa asked the other elders to speak. One by one they supported Moaula's candidacy and tried not to look at Felefele, who was by then weeping silently, and Elefane, who was gazing in shocked disbelief up into the fale dome. Moaula said that he was too inexperienced to be the next Faleasa, but, as he spoke, Faleasa sensed that he was proud to have been chosen. So, when he finished speaking Faleasa signalled to his cousin. In a short congratulatory speech his cousin ordered Moaula to accept the title, saying it was the firm wish of their aiga that he should do so. There were no further objections from Moaula.

When the meal was served at the end of the meeting Felefele immediately disappeared into one of the neighbouring fale. Elefane mumbled something about having to see somebody and marched down the road through the brilliant sunlight and sweltering heat, while they all (apart from Faleasa) tried not to watch his suffering.

As soon as everyone had left that afternoon Felefele came to Faleasa, and in a bout of controlled weeping (she spoke clearly) opposed Moaula's candidacy. Faleasa said, 'The choice of a successor is up to our aiga and they have chosen Moaula.'

'But you could change their choice,' she insisted.

Shaking his head furiously, he said, 'I won't do anything so dishonest. How could you of all people suggest such a thing? You are asking me to trample on one of the most sacred and time-honoured traditions of our beloved country. And Moaula, as well as Elefane, is your flesh and blood!' After a few more remarks of this kind he had her apologising for suggesting that he should influence their aiga's decision.

That evening Elefane and Povave and their large brood packed their possessions and caught the last bus going through Malaeiua to Povave's village on the other side of the island. A weeping Felefele pleaded with Faleasa to plead with Elefane not to leave. But Faleasa adamantly refused to do so, and said that, by behaving like a spoilt child, Elefane was showing their aiga and village that he was definitely not capable of assuming the Faleasa title.

Three nights later—and Faleasa would always remember the heavy downpour that fell, and how for a frightened moment something in the cold clatter of rain had tried to warn him—Faleasa's two eldest married daughters, Momoe and Tifaga, who for years had tried to get him to confer some of the vacant aiga titles on their husbands, visited him when no one else was about.

Their husbands had served the aiga well, they said beseechingly, and they were the only untitled men of their mature age in Malaelua. Faleasa had never felt close to his daughters: they were cold, calculating, and shrewd; their alofa was based on a disguised desire to advance their own selfish interests. Over the twenty years he had known their husbands he had pitied them because their wives controlled their lives completely. The two men had also infuriated him because they allowed their wives to rule them. But hasn't Felefele ruled my life up to now? he had to ask himself. So, as his daughters pleaded with him, he relented gradually. After all, they were his daughters; they, like Moaula, deserved some worth-while inheritance from him; he was to die soon, he had to show them his alofa; he couldn't die despising some of the fruit of his own flesh.

So he told his daughters he would do as they asked.

In the joint saofai held at the end of that month the title Faleasa was conferred on Moaula, and two less important matai titles were conferred on Faleasa's two sons-in-law.

The night of the saofai, when everyone was asleep, Faleasa woke Moaula and took him for a walk along the beach. He told Moaula to promise that he would support Laaumatua in the matai council. The only trustworthy person left in Malaelua was Laaumatua, he insisted. Moaula promised.

Just before they returned home Faleasa told Moaula that Filemoni was not a suitable pastor for Maluelua: he was stealing—there was no other word for it—village money and was therefore disgracing their aiga. Moaula was to help Laaumatua to oust Filemoni. There were also unscrupulous scoundrels who needed to be expelled from the council.

'Who?' Moaula asked.

'Laaumatua will tell you who they are,' replied Faleasa.

Chapter 4

It was 1921 when Osovae and Lemigao saw their first papalagi. He was a missionary and he was accompanied to Malaelua by two Samoan pastors and a group of youths carrying their baggage. The missionary party was visiting every village which had a London Missionary Society congregation. At that time Osovae was the leader of the pastor's school which all the young people of Malaelua except Lemigao attended. Eight years before Lemigao had refused to attend, and that was that, even though his grandparents gave him a series of beatings. But when he heard of the papalagi's visit he persuaded Osovae to let him rejoin the school at least for the duration of the papalagi's stay.

Late morning. When word spread quickly that the missionary and his party had reached the eastern outskirts of the village the young people swarmed to view him. All young Malaeluans, including Osovae and Lemigao, had heard that all papalagi were as white as wave-foam, with hair the colour of bright sunshine, and curious brown spots, that looked like fly shit, all over their bodies, especially on their faces. Papalagi were also much taller than Samoans, and they wore three layers of clothes, with rows of golden buttons, and protective covering on their feet called seevae. They carried in their pockets precious machines which told the time, lots of money, and sometimes guns which they used to kill any Samoan who offended them. So, when Osovae and Lemigao saw the missionary they couldn't quite believe he was a papalagi, because he was shorter than the Samoans who were with him, his skin was more red than white, his hair was black, there were no spots on his body, his legs were thin and hairy, he wore only a shirt and a pair of white shorts, and he didn't look impressive at all without a gun. 'Is this the papalagi?' Lemigao whispered to one of the youths accompanying the missionary. The youth didn't show in any way that he had heard the question.

After studying the missionary for a few more minutes (and the swarm of children was now thick around him), Lemigao told Osovae that the papalagi certainly didn't look tough. Osovae agreed. The papalagi's clothes were drenched with sweat, he wiped his face constantly with a large handkerchief as he walked along, smiling at everyone and with his black shoes thudding into the ground. No, the papalagi wasn't a creature to be afraid of, Osovae thought disappointedly. His father had told him that papalagi were cleverer than Samoans: they had marvellous ships and machines and books and other unbelievable possessions to prove their cleverness. But this papalagi didn't look clever at all.

Osovae and Lemigao sat with all the other young men on the paepae of the pastor's house and watched the kava ceremony of welcome. As it progressed Osovae realised that the missionary was well-versed in Samoan customs for he didn't make any mistakes in the ceremony; he didn't even look awkward sitting cross-legged on the floor. And, in the formal speeches that followed, the missionary astounded everyone with his fluency in Samoan and his oratorical power. Yes, papalagi were clever, Osovae concluded.

A large meal followed; every aiga had contributed food to it. Lemigao picked up the missionary's foodmat before anyone else could do so, limped over to him, and, smiling fearlessly at him, placed it down before him and retreated. Osovae took courage from Lemigao and carried two plates filled with corned beef and fish to the missionary. The man smiled up at him and thanked him in Samoan.

One thing the papalagi did which they had been told about was to eat nowhere near as much as Samoans and to eat it silently and slowly. Throughout the meal the papalagi conversed easily in Samoan.

That night the missionary slept behind curtains in the best Malaeluan mosquito net and on the only bed in the pastor's house, and his party slept on the floor. Osovae and

Lemigao and the other members of their class slept in the fale behind the house. As dawn melted away the dark, the pastor's wife woke them up and they cooked breakfast for the guests. The Malaeluans usually had two meals a day— one at mid-morning and one in the evening—but they had heard that papalagi had one meal in the early morning, one at midday, and one in the evening. Hence, on the advice of those elders who knew something about papalagi, the pastor's wife and the women's committee had decided the previous week that for breakfast the missionary was to be given four fried eggs, cabin bread, jam, and tea, with tinned milk and a lot of sugar. He was also to be provided with a knife and fork, so the only two forks in Malaelua—which belonged to a woman who had recently lived in Apia—were taken to the pastor's house. He must use the best crockery too, so the women's committee leaders had inspected all the crockery in the village and picked out the best.

While they were preparing breakfast the missionary emerged from the house, dressed in what looked like a woman's dress, and went into the outside shelter where the drums of drinking water were kept. As he brushed his teeth with what the pastor's wife told the young people were toothpaste and a toothbrush they all watched him. Next the missionary shaved with a silver razor and hand-mirror that sparkled in the morning light. He then returned to the house, with Osovae envying him.

The pastor's school assembled in his house at mid-morning to perform for the missionary party. As seniors, Osovae's class occupied the last row of mats. They were all dressed in their Sunday best: starched white shirts and lavalava and belts. Most of their parents occupied the edges of the large room, and on the paepae and in the shade of nearby trees were nearly all the other Malaeluan adults.

At the front, facing the school, was the missionary, sitting in the best chair in Malaelua—a cane one which had been repainted with thick white paint. Behind him, also on chairs, were his colleagues. The pastor and his wife sat on the floor in line with the missionary's chair. The missionary wore a white jacket and trousers, a white shirt and black tie, and black shoes as shiny as wet river boulders. Perched on his nose was a pair of black-rimmed spectacles. Osovae promised himself that one day he would own a suit as handsome as the missionary's.

When the missionary stood up and smiled at everyone the crowd fell silent, and only the hissing of the surf slashing at the reef brushed at Osovae's hearing. The missionary bowed his head and everyone followed his example. Then the missionary prayed in a loud voice. When he finished his prayer he smiled at everyone again, congratulated Malaelua on having one of the biggest pastors' schools in Samoa, and added that he was looking forward to seeing the students perform.

In the next two hours, and no one seemed to notice the heat, members of the pastor's school, either in classes or individually, got up in front of everyone and recited biblical verses or short sermons which the pastor and his wife had chosen or written for them to memorise. Some of the children broke down in tears and couldn't finish their recitations but the missionary only laughed good-naturedly. In between recitations the classes sang hymns. The last two hymns, sung in English by the senior class, were 'Onward Christian Soldiers' and 'Jesus Wants Me for a Sunbeam'. As he sang Osovae remembered the whippings many of them had received from the pastor while they had tried to learn these hymns which they didn't understand. During the first exciting practices he had wished to be able to speak English one day, but as the practices became more tedious and the whippings more severe he had forgotten his wish. Lemigao, who was standing beside Osovae, was pretending he knew the hymn; he was opening and shaping his mouth to what he thought the words might be. When Osovae realised this he pinched Lemigao's elbow and winked at him.

After their performance the missionary, whose once immaculate suit was now patched with sweat, congratulated them and said another prayer. Then they dispersed for the midday meal.

The school divided into three groups in the afternoon. The missionary and his two pastor colleagues were to test the students on their knowledge of the Bible, arithmetic, and reading. The missionary tested Osovae's class first. At the beginning of his interrogation no students made any mistakes. When the missionary reached Osovae he asked him to describe the story of Noah and the Flood. Half way through Osovae's fluent narration the missionary told him to stop and let the youth behind him continue the story. This was Lemigao. A still hush fell over the students. Lemigao gazed directly at the missionary as if he hadn't heard. Some of the girls started to giggle. The missionary smiled at Lemigao and repeated his request. Osovae wondered how his friend was going to get out of his predicament. To his relief and surprise Lemigao groaned sharply and began to massage his burden. The missionary rushed over to him and, holding his foot, asked him if he was all right. Lemigao nodded, and his painful groaning diminished quickly but he kept massaging his foot. The missionary comforted him and told him he would be all right. By the time the missionary returned to his seat he had forgotten his request to Lemigao, and the students were relieved that he wouldn't disgrace them in front of this very important papalagi and church leader.

When he had questioned the last student the missionary told the children that they were the brightest students he had ever tested in the country, thanked them, and moved over to the next class. One of the pastors then came to test Osovae's class in arithmetic.

Right from the start Osovae sensed that the pastor wouldn't tolerate errors: he never smiled; his squat body anchored him threateningly to the chair; his bulky head was almost clean-shaven and gleamed with hair-oil; he clutched in his right hand a supple guava-tree branch that he flicked up and down like the feared tail of a stingray. He delivered his questions in a staccato voice and they sounded more like threats than questions. Osovae began to fear for Lemigao's safety.

The fourth student questioned, a girl, gave the first wrong answer. The pastor grinned, the guava branch flicked up, the students grew more silent. The branch nipped the shoulder of a youth who gave the next wrong answer. Soon after that it stung the bare arm of another youth. Ten or so painful stings later the branch was pointing at Lemigao.

'Twelve multiplied by twelve?' the pastor asked Lemigao. No reply. The pastor repeated the question, this time slowly.

'One hundred and forty-four!' Osovae interjected. The branch moved slowly to point at him, its tip quivering almost imperceptibly.

'I didn't ask you,' the pastor said. Osovae bowed his head, hoping he had saved Lemigao. 'Twelve multiplied by eight?' the pastor asked Lemigao.

'Ninety-six!' Osovae replied for Lemigao. The branch stung his left shoulder but he continued to stare at the pastor as if he hadn't felt anything. 'Ninety-six!' he repeated. The branch stung him again, this time on his right shoulder.

'Yes, ninety-six!' Lemigao replied.

The pastor was by then trembling visibly. The branch moved towards Lemigao, hesitated, stopped, and then drooped down against the pastor's leg. He didn't even thank them when he got up a short time later to switch places with the other pastor who was to test their reading.

'Bald-headed arse!' Lemigao whispered to Osovae as the pastor moved away.

The missionary party stayed another whole day and night but Osovae and Lemigao didn't help at the pastor's house again; they didn't even bother to watch their visitors leaving. Instead they went fishing.

'Ninety-six!' Lemigao shouted as they paddled towards the reef.

'Yes, ninety-six!' yelled Osovae.

And they laughed and laughed.

That same year, three weeks before Christmas day, Osovae and Lemigao visited Apia for the first time, as members of a large Malaeluan party. There was no road to Apia from Malaelua: this and the large size of their group meant that they had to make the trip by sea on three fautasi.

Osovae's father organised and led the trip. Many of the

elders and some of their wives went, and the strongest
rowers were picked for the arduous journey, which took
them nearly three days. At night they rested in villages along
the way.

As they rounded the tip of Mulinuu peninsula and headed
into Apia harbour Osovae and Lemigao stopped rowing and
gaped at the curving seashore, at the low line and scatter of
buildings shimmering in the light against a backdrop of hills
that rolled up to the mountain range, blue and smoking and
smothering the sky's edge. From that distance Apia looked
like a vision one could touch, smell, and taste but never
quite possess.

'Row!' Osovae's father called to Osovae and Lemigao.
Osovae had persuaded his father to bring them along as
rowers. After their first nearly full day of rowing in the
blistering sun they had found it almost too painful to keep
to the rhythm Osovae's father was calling out; all their
muscles were pleading for a rest and their skin was badly
sunburnt. But when Osovae's father saw that they weren't
rowing properly he threatened never to bring them on
another Apia trip.

As they approached the jetty they sighed in amazed
disbelief. Such large boats and ships and so many buildings!
And what a size the buildings were—so high and massive
and all made of iron and stone and wood and glass! And
even from that distance they could make out crowds of
people and traffic moving up and down the main road along
the waterfront. They were eagerly awaiting their first sight
of a motor car, which they had heard was a marvellous
machine that ran on wheels, used a magic fluid called
penisini, carried loads that a hundred men couldn't carry,
and moved faster even than sharks. They were also eager—
and their hearts were by then thudding violently against
their ribs—to go into one of those stores they had heard so
many unbelievable stories about. Faleoloa—treasure
houses, one Malaeluan had called them, where you could
buy every kind of food and machine and implement you
could ever need or want.

Osovae and Lemigao were the first to jump on to the

jetty. They tied the fautasi to the jetty, and the passengers disembarked. The cargo of copra, bananas, and taro was unloaded, and Osovae's father told most of the crew to go with him and carry the copra to a nearby trading store. The rest of the crew except Osovae and Lemigao were to take the luggage and the remainder of the cargo and wait for Osovae's father and his party in the village of Apia at the other end of the town, where they were to be billeted by relatives. Osovae and Lemigao were to help carry the elders' luggage.

Loaded down with suitcases and baskets Osovae and Lemigao followed the elders down Beach Road. They stopped every few yards to absorb all the sights, and pedestrians pushed past them impatiently. When their first car, a shiny red contraption with golden plates on its wheels, roared down towards them they jumped back in fright. The car flashed past like an angry shark (that was how Lemigao described it to the young people in Malaelua when they got back), and in it they saw a papalagi family, all golden-haired and dressed in white. Then one, two, three, four more unbelievable cars went by, and the air was wild with dust and the smell of penisini, and they coughed and wiped the grit out of their eyes.

As soon as they reached their relatives' fale they dumped the luggage and hurried back to the main street. They had a pound to spend.

They stopped at the wide doorway and peered into the store which was half-filled with customers. Long rows of glass counters, in which they saw a shiny array of goods, lined the room. Behind them stood the shop assistants. All the walls of the room, right up to the ceiling, were lined with shelves stacked with more goods. In the centre of the room, stacked up against three massive posts, were barrels of salted beef, large tins of cabin bread, sacks of flour and sugar, three drums of kerosine, and racks of bushknives and other plantation tools. Ready-made dresses, shirts, and lavalava hung from the ceiling. All colours of the rainbow, Osovae observed.

Lemigao entered first. Osovae followed him hesitantly.

They moved along behind the line of customers in front of the nearest counter and looked at the goods entombed in glass. A short way down two boys pushed past them, clutching in their hands what Osovae and Lemigao immediately recognised as ice-creams: they had heard countless detailed stories about this cold sweet food. They looked about quickly; Lemigao discovered the ice-cream counter first and pointed to it.

Moving up to the counter through a thick line of customers, they stopped for a minute and watched the middle-aged man behind the counter. He was dressed in khaki shorts and a white singlet which revealed his abundant paunch hanging over a thick belt. He was scooping the white soft food out of a large paper container standing within a bigger metal container over which water vapour had collected. He pressed the ice-cream into long thin cups, round at the mouth and tapering off to a point at the end. Their mouths watered as they watched.

'Do you want anything?' asked the man, who exuded a strong smell of dried sweat.

Again Lemigao was the first to venture into the unknown. 'Two of those,' he replied, pointing at the ice-cream.

As the man scooped up the ice-cream he asked, 'You boys from the back?' Osovae and Lemigao glanced at each other, puzzled at first by the question. Osovae recognised amusement in the man's look. When they both nodded he smiled, revealing that most of his front teeth were missing.

Osovae handed the man the pound note when he received their ice-creams.

'And some of those!' Lemigao said, pointing at the jars of sweets on the shelf behind the man.

'How much?' the man asked. Lemigao didn't understand so he looked at Osovae.

'One shillings-worth,' Osovae said. The man put a handful of sweets into a paper bag and tossed it to Lemigao who caught it.

'Anything else?' the man asked. Osovae shook his head and handed Lemigao one of the ice-creams. Lemigao started to walk away, licking his ice-cream. Osovae began to follow him. 'Your change!' the man called. As the man counted the change into his palm Osovae avoided looking into his amused smile.

By the time Osovae caught up to Lemigao on the front veranda his friend had nearly finished his ice-cream. 'Really beautiful, really beautiful,' he murmured, licking his lips and gazing at the remainder of his ice-cream. Osovae's tongue stabbed out quickly and tasted the sweet running coldness; he nodded his head and bit into the white succulence. The cold stung his teeth to their very roots.

They bought two more ice-creams from the next store and went and sat under a pulu tree near the sea wall where they ate their ice-creams and observed the traffic of people and vehicles. As they got up to continue their exploration of the town Osovae remembered that they hadn't asked the price of the ice-creams; he also remembered the many tales he'd heard of Apia being a den of thieves; so he put their change on the ground and counted it carefully.

'Well?' Lemigao asked.

'No, boy from the back,' said Osovae, 'they didn't cheat us!' (Not knowing the correct price of an ice-cream, they would never know if they had been cheated or not, he told himself.)

A short time later, dripping with sweat from the heat, which seemed to shimmer up from the foundations of the town, they found themselves in what they concluded, after studying the crowds milling around food stalls under the high corrugated iron dome of the biggest building they had ever seen, must be the Apia market. Many of the men were dressed in tattered shirts or singlets and khaki shorts; the women wore short dresses which revealed their legs immodestly; some of the people wore shoes or sandals.

After walking round the market, examining all the food and goods, and listening attentively to the bargaining, they concluded that the Samoan spoken by the inhabitants of Apia was quaint, unusual—they used the k instead of the t. Perhaps it had something to do with the language of the papalagi, surmised Osovae.

Lemigao said he was hungry so they bought some baked

taro and palusami and octopus cooked in coconut cream. This time Osovae asked the price before buying. They sat on the grass under a sprawling mango tree behind the market and began to eat silently. When they had finished the octopus Lemigao said that he was still hungry so Osovae gave him some money. He bought a tin of corned beef, which they opened with a bushknife lent to them by a nearby aiga. They shared the corned beef with the aiga.

Shortly afterwards Lemigao stretched out on the grass, with his hands clasped over his well-rounded belly, and began to drift off to sleep. But Osovae glanced up at the sky through a gap in the tangled foliage of the mango tree and could see from the sun's position that it was past noon. He suddenly remembered having heard that in Apia Samoans followed the papalagi practice of having three meals a day, and that they should be with the elders, serving them their midday meal. He shook Lemigao roughly, pulled him up when he rolled over and refused to wake, told him it was late, and hurried off, with Lemigao trailing him and complaining loudly.

The elders were having their meal in the main fale when Osovae and Lemigao got back and joined the group of untitled men and women who were serving the food. No one said anything to them, and Osovae hoped his father hadn't noticed their absence.

All the elders and most of the older untitled men went to sleep not long after their meal. But before sleeping Osovae's father sent for him, ordered him to stop setting such a bad example to the other young men, and said they were to make a big umu for the evening meal. When Osovae told Lemigao and the other youths they complained.

So, in the inescapable heat, their bodies aching from their long journey, they sweated and complained—but not too loudly in case their elders heard—as they made the umu. Lemigao tried to cheer them up by describing in vivid but exaggerated detail their experiences in the town that morning. He stopped when he realised no one was listening to him.

Late in the afternoon, after they had covered the umu with

banana leaves and wet sacks, they found some old mats, spread them out in the shade of a clump of bananas near the kitchen fale, and went to sleep.

One of the elders woke them just as the sun was drowning in the mountains to the west. They were still tired, too tired to feel elated any more about being in Apia, the heart of the papalagi's mysterious world—the new world, as one elder had called it the previous day.

That evening when they went to shower they discovered tap water, although it wasn't really a discovery because, like many other Apia wonders, they had often been told about it. They spent a long time enjoying the cool fingers of water stabbing down at their bodies, and Lemigao insisted on turning the tap off and on to see how it worked. That same evening, straight after lotu in the main fale, they experienced the mystery of electric light. (Brighter than daylight, as Lemigao later described it.) During the remainder of their three-day stay they made other discoveries. These discoveries became the basis of stories, exaggerated or otherwise, that they, especially Lemigao, dazzled the young people of Malaelua with on their return, just as those who had visited Apia before them had dazzled them with stories.

On their first night the elders and the aualuma of Apia visited them with gifts of food and there was feasting and dancing late into the night.

All the Malaeluan youths helped the Apia women serve the food. While they were serving, Lemigao, without anyone noticing, pinched Osovae's arm and whispered that a beautiful girl was eyeing him. Osovae refused to believe him. 'Over there,' said Lemigao, pointing. For a little while Osovae refused to look. Then, when Lemigao had turned away, he glanced across for an instant, and before she could look away he saw a pretty girl of about his own age gazing at him. From then on he felt he was being watched and he was pleased about it.

As the girl passed him in order to deliver a foodmat to one of the elders he noticed that she was of mixed blood: fair skinned and with very papalagi features. When the feast was over and they were packing away the dishes and leftovers he whispered as he passed her, 'Can I see you later on?' A few minutes later, as she passed him, she shook her head.

When she and a few other Apia girls stood up to dance Osovae sprang up also; two other Malaelua youths joined him and they danced with the girls. 'Can I see you tonight?' he whispered as he danced near her. Just before she sat down at the back of the group of singers she nodded to him. He danced over, sat down behind her, and clapped and sang. 'Where?' he asked her as the song ended. She didn't speak to him for the rest of the festivities, but her presence enveloped him and he felt like he had felt that morning as they approached Apia and it had seemed like a vision he could smell, touch, and taste but never quite possess. Then, as she rose to leave with a group of friends, she motioned to him to meet her outside.

He slipped out of the fale as the crowd dispersed, his senses alert, for he knew it would be fatal for him if Apia youths found him courting one of their women.

The girls stopped a safe distance from the fale and she walked back towards him. She was to be his first Apia conquest, he congratulated himself, as the girl, barely visible in the darkness, stopped a few feet away and he smelt her heady perfume.

'Why did you want to see me?' she asked.

'I just wanted to talk to you,' he replied. 'Tell your friends to leave us alone.'

'Why?'

'Don't you want to be alone with me?' She giggled. He reached out and touched her arm. She didn't move away and he was sure he would win her.

'So go on and talk to me,' she challenged, trying to suppress a bout of laughter.

'What's your name?' He caressed her arm.

'I haven't got one,' she said. 'I have to go now.

'But why?'

'My aiga will be searching for me soon.'

'May I see you tomorrow night?' he asked, holding her arm.

'I'll meet you behind the LMS church about this time,' she

promised, pulling her arm away and running off to join her friends.

As the girls disappeared into the darkness he heard them laughing; her laughter had a mysterious, haunting quality.

The following night he waited for her behind the church. She didn't come. He waited again the next night. She didn't come. He was never to see her again.

On their way back to Malaelua Lemigao joked about it. Osovae told him to shut up.

Throughout his life, whenever he visited Apia, he remembered her, especially her haunting laughter. He would never be able to quite admit to himself that she had been laughing at him. She was that mysterious quality of Apia that kept eluding him.

Chapter 5

In the middle of 1942 Lemigao, who was still without a permanent wife, disappeared from Malaelua. Osovae worried about him until he reappeared just before Christmas day dressed in faded military trousers, a white T-shirt, and army boots, and carrying a huge duffle bag fat with packets of sugar and rice, all sorts of tinned meat, cartons of American cigarettes, chewing gum, which he gave the children who crowded round him as soon as he got off the bus, chocolate bars, which he gave Osovae's toothless mother, more T-shirts which he gave Osovae and his other friends, and a roll of American dollars, out of which he gave five dollars to the pastor, a dollar each to all the matai who visited him his first night home, ten dollars to Osovae's wife, and the rest to his grandparents, who now told everyone that Lemigao had always been their most dutiful, most generous son.

When they were alone that night Lemigao told Osovae that he had been working at the new American Air Base at Faleolo just over the mountain range. He vividly described what he had seen and done. Americans, or Yanks as he called them, unlike the mean New Zealanders who were ruling their country, were the most generous papalagi in the world. Because they were also the richest people in the world they were bound to win the war. As Lemigao spoke Osovae noticed that his language was peppered with English words. Osovae didn't know what the words meant but he didn't say so.

At that time money was needed to build a new school in Malaelua, so when Lemigao asked Osovae if he wanted to work for the Yanks for a few months he agreed readily. The next day forty other men also agreed to work at the Base. The Samoan workers lived in a group of fale which the

Americans had built under rows of lush palms a short distance from the edge of the airfield. The Malaeluan party was given the largest fale. Lemigao boasted to Osovae that he had some influence with the American sergeant in charge of the Malaeluans.

On their first morning, just before they started work, Lemigao told them that the Yankee sergeant had appointed Osovae to be their overseer. He also told them, if they finished digging a hundred yards of the ditch by the end of that week they would receive bonuses; because of his burden he was to help in the kitchen. So, while the Malaeluan party worked in the blazing sun, Lemigao worked in the shade of the enormous kitchen, but they didn't grudge him this privilege because he returned every night with extra food to supplement their free meals, and sometimes with a whole carton of tinned food to share and take home to their aiga, with chocolate bars, cigarettes, biscuits and sweets, pots and pans and other kitchen ware for their wives. No one dared ask if he had stolen them. So every week-end when they went home they had generous gifts from the generous Yanks (Lemigao's description) for their wives and children. Lemigao's grandparents usually received the most generous of these gifts.

The only American they got to know well was the sergeant. It was he who, through his Samoan interpreter, gave them their orders, listened to their problems, and paid them at the end of each week. He was a pudgy little man who in his mannerisms reminded Osovae of an overgrown puppy. He never got angry with them and sometimes after eating with them played cards with them late into the night. Through his interpreter they learnt that he had a wife and four children, was a carpenter by trade, had been drafted into the Marines four years before and hated army life but thought Samoa the most beautiful group of islands he had ever visited. This last claim endeared him still more to them.

Because the interpreter was their main means of communicating with the sergeant they also got to know him. His name was Samu but they referred to him among themselves as Fuamiti-Laiti, Tiny-Testicles, because they disliked him intensely. He was too officious and arrogant in his long socks and shoes, white shorts and shirt—the picture of a black bastard trying to be a papalagi bastard, was Lemigao's description of him. At night, when the sergeant and the interpreter weren't about, Lemigao delighted the Malaeluans with his hilariously accurate imitations of the interpreter.

Just over a month after they started work at the Base, the interpreter reported to the sergeant that Lemigao was stealing army property. The sergeant acted as if he hadn't heard. When the interpreter repeated his accusation the sergeant asked him if he was a Samoan or not. The meaning of the question escaped the interpreter and he began to detail Lemigao's thefts but the sergeant simply walked away. The following morning the interpreter asked the sergeant if anything was going to be done about Lemigao. They needed proof, the sergeant dismissed him.

The next Friday evening, while Osovae and Lemigao were packing their bags for the week-end and the sergeant was playing cards with some of the other men, the interpreter came in and before anyone saw what he was doing reached into Lemigao's duffle bag, pulled out a handful of army knives and forks, and placed them in front of the sergeant. He glanced at them and then at the interpreter and went on playing as if nothing had happened, while the interpreter just stood, crucified to the silence by the hostile stares of the Malaeluans. A minute later he bowed his head, gave the sergeant one last desperate look, turned, and almost ran out of the fale.

Some hours later, when they had finished their card game, the sergeant picked up the cutlery, looked at it for a moment, then looked across at Lemigao, smiled as he handed the cutlery to Osovae, and left, yawning loudly.

On the Monday morning the sergeant arrived at work with a new interpreter. Nothing was ever again said about the incident.

None of them would be able to remember exactly when the sergeant started bringing bottles of beer to their fale, and then, as more and more of them began drinking with him, whole cartons, and then bottles of bourbon. But Osovae would remember years afterwards that it had coincided with the news of large numbers of American marines who had been stationed at Faleolo being killed in the Solomon Islands and New Guinea.

At first only Lemigao drank with the sergeant. Then Lemigao persuaded a few others to. Eventually only Osovae and three other men, who were deacons, did not drink. The card games turned into singing and dancing and rowdily laughing affairs, punctuated by fist fights, which Osovae had to stop. The sergeant, Osovae observed, enjoyed encouraging the fist fights. One night, after a particularly heavy drinking bout, the sergeant took out his wallet and, weeping like a child, showed the Malaeluans a photograph of his wife and children. When he fell asleep Osovae and two other men carried him to his quarters. Not many nights after that he burst into their fale at midnight, kicked them awake, order- ed them to drink with him, and—while guzzling from the bottle and with the liquid slopping over his chin and clothes —wept and raved. Because they didn't understand English they couldn't fathom the cause of his anguish. He was like a person possessed by a demon which had to be placated con- stantly with drink, or by a fire which raged and couldn't be extinguished, Osovae said. Someone else suggested that the sergeant was lonely for his family and his beloved country.

Not long after, while the sergeant was again drunk and weeping uncontrollably, Osovae got the interpreter to trans- late what the sergeant was saying, but as soon as he saw the interpreter he ordered him to get out. Osovae got the inter- preter a second time but again the sergeant ordered him to leave. Osovae concluded that the sergeant didn't want them to know the root of his pain. So he didn't try again; the ser- geant was their friend and they must respect his wishes.

On their way back from Malaelua the following Sunday afternoon Lemigao diagnosed the sergeant's malady as loneliness and prescribed a succulent woman as the cure. Osovae at first pretended shock, then concurred. Lemigao immediately suggested that they should take the sergeant with them to Malaelua the next week-end and persuade one of their women to *heal* him. 'And get ourselves into serious trouble?' replied Osovae. 'No. It must be done well away from Malaelua.' One of the prostitutes who came to the Base at the week-ends, Lemigao said, should do the job well. Osovae was silent for a while and then asked if Lemigao had ever seen the sergeant with any of these loose women. (He couldn't make himself say prostitute.) Lemigao pondered and then shook his head. 'It must be a woman who will heal out of a sense of compassion and not for money,' Osovae said. 'But who?' asked Lemigao. Osovae told Lemigao to scout round the Base for a suitable woman. 'Why me?' retorted Lemigao. Trying not to burst into triumphant laughter, Osovae said, 'Because you are the only one working at the centre of all the Base's activities. You are the most logical choice.'

Before Lemigao went off to the kitchen on the Monday morning he pleaded with Osovae to reconsider their plan: after all they were going to make a respectably married man commit the heinous sin of adultery. 'The whole idea was yours in the first place,' Osovae reminded him. Lemigao immediately sought refuge in his burden, claiming that no woman ever looked at him because of his club-foot. 'Liar!' said Osovae, moving off before Lemigao could say any more.

For almost a week Lemigao kept telling Osovae that he hadn't yet found a suitable woman. During that time the sergeant was drunk only once in their fale and Osovae thought he was getting better. Then on the Friday night, immediately after their evening meal, a jeep roared up and screeched to a halt; out of it tumbled the sergeant, drunk, and with his face bloody and alive with cuts and bruises. He stumbled into the fale, fell on to his stomach, and started beating at the floor with his fists. Someone brought a basin of water and pieces of cloth, and Osovae and Lemigao turned him over and cleaned the blood off his face. Soon he fell asleep and Osovae covered him with a sheet. When they woke in the morning he had gone. At work the following Monday the Malaeluans behaved as though nothing had happened and tried not to look at the cuts and bruises on the sergeant's face.

Then the sergeant suddenly stopped visiting the fale at night, was unusually cheerful at work, and as far as they knew had stopped drinking. After a week of this Osovae told Lemigao that there was no longer any need to find a cure for their friend because he had obviously healed himself. Chuckling, Lemigao told him that their friend was curing himself with a lively cure he had arranged. They both laughed. 'Who is she?' Osovae asked, but Lemigao evaded the question by saying he had heard that the Yanks were now beating the excrement out of the Japanese in the Solomon Islands.

One night, only a fortnight before they would finish their work at the Base and return home permanently, Osovae was trying to sleep; but the night was still and the heat clung tenaciously. Around him the other men tossed and turned noisily in their sleep. Lemigao's sleeping place, he noticed, was empty. After some minutes, as his friend didn't return, Osovae swept off his sleeping sheet and left the fale quietly.

The bright moonlight made everything outside the colour of glistening lead. As he strolled through the group of fale he could hear the barking of dogs coming from the direction of the rubbish dump a short distance behind the Base; the dull throbbing of the surf also tugged at his hearing. He stopped in the shadow of a palm and urinated into the ground. A rat scuffled across the dry palm fronds lying behind him. He looked round. The shadows seemed to be crouching, ready to pounce on him. He fought his fear, refused to return to the fale, and walked down the slight slope and across the tarmac towards the narrow beach at the western end of the airfield.

He had often gone to the beach at night to sit and think and watch the waves sliding smoothly on to the sand; it had always been deserted; but tonight he sensed that other people were there, and he approached it cautiously.

Suddenly he heard Lemigao laugh. He stopped, and for a moment nearly went back; but, as he listened to Lemigao's easy laughter and thought of the uncomfortable heat in the fale, he decided to go on. He paused again when he heard the high-pitched laughter of a woman and the sergeant's deeper laughter. Then, remembering that Lemigao had arranged a woman for the sergeant, curiosity overcame his reluctance to intrude. He crouched down and crawled up to the low line of discarded palm trunks overlooking the beach.

Three figures lay sprawled a few feet apart on the sand, only a short distance away; the woman—and he couldn't recognise her in the moonlight—was lying in the middle, and they were passing a bottle round and swigging from it. Occasionally they laughed and slapped one another. Suddenly the sergeant, who was bare to the waist, his torso looking yellow in the moonlight, sprang up and danced a few steps forward and back while his companions clapped out the rhythm. As they clapped faster he danced faster, flailing his arms wildly in the air, his head pumping backwards and forwards in time to the beat, his short legs thumping like pistons into the sand, haunting whimpers issuing from between his clenched teeth. He looked as if he couldn't stop the hypnotic dance, as if to do so would topple him into a bottomless chasm. Osovae wanted to stop Lemigao and the woman from beating out the frantic rhythm, but just before he could get up and run forward the sergeant wrapped his arms round his head, collapsed to his knees, and rocked back and forth, weeping mutedly. Osovae realised then, with profound sadness, that he could not interfere. His friend would never forgive him if he stopped him from enjoying his self-destructive pain, his exhilarating dance in death's embrace.

As soon as Osovae saw the woman rise slowly to her feet and advance drunkenly towards the sergeant, dragging her feet in the sand, he realised that their prescribed cure for the sergeant's malady had been a tragic error. He tried to force himself away from what he sensed was going to happen but found that he couldn't. His whole being was alive like a hungry cannibal flower.

The woman stopped directly in front of the sergeant, unpinned her hair, which tumbled down her back, and then, with exaggerated movements, like those of a slow dance, undressed until she was completely naked, the light like an unforgiving rash on her skin. The sergeant stopped whimpering as she stepped up and stood with her thighs touching his face. She parted her legs, held the back of his head roughly, pushed his face between her thighs, and then moved her hips in a circular motion while she made a low continuous moaning sound. Lemigao, who was now on his knees, watched and clapped out the rhythm again. As he clapped faster and the woman's hips rotated more quickly he moved forward, still on his knees, until his face was pressing against her buttocks.

Abruptly Lemigao stopped clapping and toppled back on to the sand. Then the woman was on top of him, her hands clawing at his chest, her hips pumping up and down, as she made violent love to him, while the sergeant knelt beside them, watching and clapping feebly, encouraging them.

The woman tensed, flung back her head, and gasped loudly. Osovae recognised her then. She was one of the young prostitutes who visited the Base every week-end.

He turned and stumbled away to the fale. For the rest of the night he couldn't sleep.

Lemigao crawled into the fale as dawn broke.

The Malaeluans never saw the sergeant again. A few days later they were told that he had been transferred to the Solomon Islands at his own request.

Osovae never told anyone what he had witnessed, but for a long time afterwards, when Lemigao came near him, he felt bitter anger mixed with an inexplicable fear, as though Lemigao's presence was accusing him of a terrible crime he had committed or confronting him with a monstrous side of himself that he was too afraid to accept.

Chapter 6

Just before noon Faleasa and Laaumatua reached the small fale in the middle of Faleasa's cacao plantation. A thick cover of cloud hid the sun, so it was pleasantly warm, with a slow breeze flowing like a sea of green plankton through the lush cacao trees that were heavy with fruit. They were both breathing hard from their walk as they entered the fale and Moaula spread some mats for them to sit on. 'My creaky skeleton won't take much more of this,' sighed Faleasa. For a while they remained silent trying to recover their breath. Moaula, who had arrived before them to prepare a meal, asked if they were ready to eat. Laaumatua nodded eagerly, and within minutes Moaula placed foodmats before them. On the mats, their delicious odour filling the fale, were pieces of taro cooked with coconut cream, large pieces of chicken roasted over charcoal, and steaming mugs of home-made cocoa. Laaumatua glanced impatiently at Faleasa who had shut his eyes to say grace; and then, as usual, he was into the food before Faleasa's eyes were fully open.

Faleasa wasn't hungry; he just picked at his food and observed his friend. He had never ceased to marvel at the way Laaumatua devoured his food. There was a definite style about it: perfect and almost total concentration; an attack which you couldn't quite brand as the rapacious style of the glutton because it was executed in silence, slowly, methodically. First he broke the taro and chicken into small pieces; then his right hand delivered each piece to his mouth with a flowing, graceful movement. In between the medium-sized mouthfuls, which he chewed thoroughly, he drank some cocoa, smiled or said something to Faleasa, and then continued. Moaula replenished his foodmat with taro and chicken twice. And, as was the custom, Laaumatua remembered to leave some food on his foodmat at the end of his meal. When it came to food Faleasa lightheartedly described his friend as 'the best-mannered, aristocratic glutton in Samoa'.

After Moaula had gone into the plantation to work and Laaumatua had washed his hands and mouth, Faleasa asked him to describe everything that had happened that week concerning the matai council and Filemoni. For the next hour or so Laaumatua did just that in elaborate detail.

He had visited Sau on Monday night, pretending that he wanted a game of cards. They played late into the night, and Laaumatua deliberately lost ninety-nine per cent of the games to Sau. (There was nothing like an orgy of victories to relax a vain man's defences.) In victory Sau was a generous, magnanimous host who woke up his wife and daughters well past midnight to cook them some pancakes and cocoa. While racing his host through the mound of pancakes Laaumatua had let fall the enticing claim that Filemoni— the arrogant nephew of Faleasa who was now insane as punishment from God for his sins—wasn't carrying out his pastoral duties properly. Sau immediately agreed and emphasised Laaumatua's claim that Faleasa's insanity was a just and holy punishment. Laaumatua had further said that Filemoni was only an immature boy whom Faleasa had foisted on them as their pastor; and, to humiliate them even more, Filemoni was dishonest. Dishonest? Sau asked. Maybe he shouldn't have mentioned it but it was costing him sleepless nights knowing what their pastor was doing, Laaumatua replied. Sau clucked his tongue in sympathy. But who was more appropriate to confess it to than the new leader of the council, Laaumatua had continued, with his head bowed but his eyes observing Sau's every reaction. Now that Faleasa was sick (and he deserved to be sick) he, Sau, the most able and generous and just matai in Malaelua, was Faleasa's natural successor. In age and education and in length of devoted service to Malaelua he was the most senior matai. He also held the highest-ranking title in Malaelua—Faleasa and his father had usurped that status. By the time he had finished flattering Sau the bait was lodged firmly in his host's vainglorious guts, Laaumatua told Faleasa, who chuckled merrily and asked his friend to go on. 'Why is our pastor dishonest?' Sau had asked eventually. 'Dishonest?' Laaumatua pretended he had forgotten. Yes Sau prompted; he, Laaumatua, had mentioned something about Filemoni's dishonesty, and as he, Sau, was now the council leader he had the right to know what their pastor was up to. As Laaumatua itemised the amounts of Malaelua money that Filemoni had spent and was still spending on his aiga, Sau, inflated with self-righteous anger, muttered something about not being able to trust even pastors in these days of darkness. By the end of Laaumatua's detailed analysis of Filemoni's illegal spending Sau was threatening impeachment of that dishonest boy, that arrogant nephew of that arrogant madman. 'Summon a council meeting!' he ordered Laaumatua. 'Yes, sir!' Laaumatua replied.

Before Laaumatua left he had convinced the new, self-appointed council leader that the meeting must be held the following day and that he must not reveal to anyone the source of his explosive information—it would be more effective for him to give the council the impression that he, their most alert leader, had investigated the matter alone and secretly.

'Creatures like Sau lack a self-healing sense of humour,' Laaumatua said to Faleasa.

'Sau should have been a modern pastor, all vanity and no testicles,' replied Faleasa; and they laughed together.

The next morning Laaumatua sent for Moaula and told him what to say at the council meeting. Moaula in turn rehearsed the matai of his aiga.

When Laaumatua arrived at Sau's fale that afternoon for the meeting he found that Sau had done his job efficiently: every matai was present; the atmosphere was tense; and, as he had expected, Sau was occupying the most important post, which, by rank, Faleasa or the holder of that title usually occupied. Laaumatua had instructed Moaula, who now held the Faleasa title, to ignore Sau's arrogant move, as his enjoyment of power would be brief.

As soon as the formal greetings were over Laaumatua

glanced at Sau, who nodded, coughed, and was into what Malaeluans later agreed was his most dazzling speech.

Sau's voice was a courageous sword which cut at, trimmed, and shaped their emotions, and, just before he killed Filemoni's reputation with it, even clanged with sorrow, so that the matai felt that he wasn't enjoying what he was about to do. As the sword, poetically but ruthlessly, carved the word T-H-I-E-F on Filemoni's absent forehead Sau even blinked a tear or two from his eyes. After the branding, which had shocked everyone (except Laaumatua and Moaula) into silence, Sau declared that, as Almighty God was his witness, he didn't harbour any personal hatred of Filemoni, that he hadn't really wanted to expose the completely unworthy behaviour of this Servant of God but had done so because he placed God and the interests of his beloved village above everything else, even above his own unworthy life.

During Sau's attack, the other matai had scruitinised Moaula because he was Filemoni's cousin and, because they well knew his quick temper, they expected him to react violently. Most of them sighed deeply when, straight after Sau's devastating oration, Moaula supported his accusations and said that Filemoni should be banished. The other matai of Moaula's aiga also advocated immediate banishment of their cousin. Sau congratulated Moaula and these matai on their courage and said that the most heart-rending thing any human being had to do was to pronounce sentence on a dear relative. One by one the other matai agreed to the punishment. And Vaelupa, who was sitting on Sau's right (it was evident to Laaumatua that the filariasis-ridden Vaelupa had already assumed the role of chief adviser to Sau, the new council leader), summed up:

'Tainted by the greed of this sinful world, and dominated by Satan, our Servant of God has committed a crime against God. For that—and this humble person for one is finding it almost too painful to say it—Filemoni, may God forgive him, must pay the supreme penalty. From this day forth he is no longer part of our beloved village.'

Vaelupa continued in this poetic vein until he realised that he was starting to bore his captive audience, so he ended: 'This unworthy person is positive that God, our most just and merciful Father, has, through us His humble servants, revealed His will concerning one of His wayward ministers. Blessings on this meeting.'

Sau's aiga then brought in a sumptuous meal, and, just before Sau said grace, Laaumatua, in his only utterance at the meeting, reminded them that no one had been appointed to convey the council's decision to Filemoni. Vaelupa volunteered to do so.

That night, when Vaelupa told Filemoni the decision, the pastor almost assaulted him and ordered him out of his house, declaring loudly that he hadn't committed any such crime and anyone who said so was the lying son of a stinking pig. Sau immediately summoned another council meeting for the next morning. Laaumatua didn't attend but he sent Moaula with instructions to influence the council into going to Filemoni's house. In front of the council and all Malaelua, Laaumatua said, Moaula was then to censure his cousin and order him to leave Malaelua.

'. . . And, as you know, Filemoni and his aiga are leaving today,' Laaumatua ended his narrative.

'Well done! I never knew you had it in you though,' said Faleasa jokingly.

'Had what?'

'The instinct of the killer!' laughed Faleasa.

'I've always had it hidden in my burden!'

They planned their next major move and then slept until late afternoon. As they walked back to Malaelua Laaumatua asked Faleasa if he had another pastor in mind. 'Did he?' Faleasa replied. Laaumatua nodded. 'So. Go ahead and get him,' Faleasa said.

Chapter 7

At first the gogo was a silver speck floating lazily in the brilliant sky; then, as Faleasa watched it, his breath propping it up in the still air, it dropped lower and lower until it was a luminous humming of outstretched wings circling above the heads of the trees he was standing under. Once, twice, three times it circled, sleek head and body pinned back, long tail trailing.... The snapping sound of his clap cracked through the dense bush. The bird hesitated in mid-air, then climbed and fled for the safety of the mountain range. Why had he frightened it away, he asked himself a moment later, as he picked a path through the undergrowth towards the river.

The river's roar broke through the trees, and he smelt its fecund odour of silt and decay and water. A few minutes later he was gazing down at its swift current, weaving and turning, and faintly brown with silt. He was sweating freely: the air was humid, he had walked a long way from Malaelua, and on the latter half of his trek he had had to cut a trail through the bush. Small clouds of mosquitoes started coming to life around him. He escaped them by moving upstream where the water was shallow and clear and still. Scooping up handfuls of water, he drank thirstily as he waded to the little island in the middle of the stream. A small stand of trees smothered with creepers covered the island. He found shade under a tree that leant over the water and sat down on a boulder. The water was bristling with noonday sun and for a moment the flashing light stunned his eyes. But, as he tolerated the pain, he grew accustomed to the light.

His father had once brought him to that spot when he was a boy, and they had spent the day fishing for shrimp. Now he was a man and his mother was dead and he didn't feel any sorrow. First she had been a burden to his father; then, when his father died, almost ten years earlier, she became his special burden—a burden he was ashamed of but had borne because she was his mother. In death she was an even heavier burden than in life.

It had all started while he was away in Apia. Vaipaia, his mother, saw some youths of the Aiga Tapu, their neighbours, planting coconut saplings on what she believed was Faleasa land, and she ordered them to stop. They ignored her. Enraged by this, she shouted insults at them. Tapu's youngest son told her to shut her toothless gob and go back to her aiga who were all descendants of nobodies. (At least, this was what she later told Faleasa the youth had said.) Her aiga restrained her and brought her back into the fale where she wailed loudly, claiming that no one in her aiga cared enough for her good name and the good name of their aiga to avenge the insult which Tapu's aiga had so cruelly inflicted on her.

That night some youths of her aiga caught Tapu's son, beat him senseless, and left him beside the pool. Later Tapu came, stood in front of their main fale, and yelled that they, the Aiga Faleasa, were all cowards. The men scrambled up to go out and accept Tapu's challenge but Vaipaia stopped them. So for the next half hour or so they had to angrily tolerate Tapu's insults as he cut down with his bushknife all their taro and banana crops which bordered the road. Faleasa would pay Tapu back, Vaipaia tried to console them. Her son, she claimed, was afraid of no one.

Faleasa had returned at noon the next day. She told him what had happened, put the entire blame on Tapu and his aiga, and demanded that he should repay in kind Tapu's insult to their dignity. When Faleasa refused to act immediately she wept and claimed that even her only son didn't love her (and their aiga) enough to avenge her honour (and the honour of their aiga). Faleasa said that the matai council would settle the matter. She wept more abundantly. He consulted the other elders in their aiga and they all agreed with Vaipaia, saying that they must attack Tapu's aiga and show their village that the Aiga Faleasa were not cowards. 'The council will settle the matter,' Faleasa said again.

That night Vaipaia refused to eat and said that she was feeling ill. They were used to her many illnesses, so Felefele bathed her in warm water and covered her with a blanket. She fell asleep and they didn't worry about her any more. During the night she woke soaked with a cold sweat and demanded to be taken to the Malaelua medical station. 'We'll take you in the morning,' Faleasa said soothingly, and she fell asleep again. A little later she became delirious with fever and her frail body shivered violently. They rushed her to the medical station; the doctor diagnosed influenza; he told them he would keep her at the station and she would be all right in a day or so. But she grew steadily worse. At the end of the week Felefele rushed from the station to tell Faleasa that Vaipaia was in a critical condition. When he reached the station the doctor told him that his mother must be taken into the Apia hospital as she was seriously ill with pneumonia.

Faleasa sat beside her while they waited for the bus to take her into the hospital. She died without recognising him.

A rumour spread through Malaelua that Vaipaia had died of a broken heart because her only son had refused to avenge her honour. Faleasa realised that he couldn't avoid his duty any longer. Even if the council punished Tapu and his aiga, he, personally, must publicly exact punishment or else his courage would always be suspect in Malaelua. If he died exacting that punishment it didn't matter: the future didn't concern the truly brave; to be branded a coward was a worse death.

His aiga would not bury Vaipaia until he returned from his trek upriver.

He took off his lavalava, placed it on the boulder, and waded into the stream until the water was up to his armpits; then he lay back and floated in the almost stationary current. The coolness invaded his every pore and healed the aching in his muscles, and for a long time he forgot his fear that he lacked the courage needed to commit that violent act that would re-establish his reputation as a brave man. The bush seemed to be watching him; occasionally a bird flew across the river.

As far back as he could remember, his mother hadn't been like the mothers of his friends. She was always tired, always claiming that she didn't understand why she hadn't the energy to do this or that. Most of the time she enveloped herself in a wary silence as if she suspected everybody and everything were trying to harm her. As a result she rarely did anything for herself; she even let his father and the women in their aiga take over his upbringing. Among Malaeluans she was labelled an idle, arrogant woman who, because she was the wife of the leading matai, treated other Malaeluans as her personal servants. The only times she roused herself enough to communicate with Osovae were when she was angry with him. So she remained almost a total stranger to him, someone he had to bear with and respect because she had given birth to him. His father inevitably became the centre round which his whole existence revolved, and, like his father, he grew ashamed of her and refused to believe people who told him that his mother had been the most vivacious girl in their district.

His father was angry with her again and again. He castigated her for what he branded as her laziness and said that he had wasted his life by marrying her. Osovae always agreed with his father, and when he was old enough to realise that his father was having affairs with other women he was glad for him.

When Osovae's father died Vaipaia emerged from her cocoon of suffering silence and filled his days with detailed complaints about her aiga not loving her. She was constantly ill, and even though he suspected her ailments were attempts to gain her aiga's affection he instructed everyone to cater to her every wish. Once, when Felefele, on whom fell the onerous task of caring for her, complained angrily that she was tired of Vaipaia's nagging, he ordered her never again to complain about his mother; as his wife it was her duty to do everything his mother wanted.

Vaipaia's insatiable dissatisfaction with everything became mirrored in her physical appearance. As she aged, her flesh and skin shrank tightly around her skeleton, strangling it, until she was a wizened, toothless gnome, her face a wrinkled fist of bitterness, her rheumy eyes clouded with cataracts. Even their aiga's children were afraid of her. Faleasa ended by resenting her appearance: he was ashamed to have so ugly a woman for his mother.

He washed his face with handfuls of water, climbed to the bank, and sat in the sun to dry himself. Only God knew how he had really felt about his mother. All dutiful sons loved their parents: that was how he had been brought up. But surely, he thought, God would forgive him, because it had been his mother's fault that he couldn't love her.

When he was dry he put on his lavalava. He would return to Malaelua and bury her in the style befitting her age and the status of his aiga; then he would right the grievous wrong Tapu's aiga had inflicted on his aiga. That was his duty. On his way home the fear that he might lack the necessary courage troubled him again.

The day after his mother's funeral he disappeared from Malaelua. The next Sunday afternoon a bus coming from Apia stopped in front of his fale and he got out. In his right hand he carried what looked like a thick yoke wrapped up in a lavalava. When his children crowded round him noisily he ordered them to go away. He went into the fale, hid the long parcel under the one bed, and told Felefele to get him some food. Throughout the meal he refused to talk to anyone.

Early the next morning he woke before anyone else, dressed in a lavalava and singlet, took the long parcel from under the bed and a small packet out of his suitcase, made sure no one in his aiga was awake, and then walked slowly towards Tapu's main fale, which was only a short distance away.

Some pigs and chickens were foraging in the shallow ditches by the road and everything was covered with dew. He stopped on the road and turned to face Tapu's fale. Its blinds were down. He knew Tapu well; they considered each other to be friends; but now that must be put aside.

Slowly he unwrapped the long parcel, revealing a shotgun which gleamed dully in the soft morning light. He didn't hesitate, afraid that any hesitation would allow fear to stop him from committing the act that his aiga and his village expected of him. The smaller packet was a box of ammunition. He tore it open, took out a cartridge, and loaded the shotgun. Then, raising the shotgun in one quick movement to his shoulder, he fired at the thatched dome of Tapu's fale. Rows of blinds were quickly pushed open and members of Tapu's aiga peered fearfully at him. He reloaded. This time he aimed at the fale's centre post which he could see through a raised row of blinds. The shot tore a spray of splinters off the post. Many of Tapu's aiga were now scrambling out and escaping into nearby fale; a baby started to shriek. A crowd had gathered on both sides of Faleasa but at a safe distance. When he saw Felefele trying to break away from the relatives who were holding her he called to her to go home.

'Tapu!' he shouted, 'come out!' A row of blinds at the western end of the fale was pushed open and Tapu stepped out to stand on the uppermost tier of the paepae. He was much older than Faleasa; he was one of the most influential matai in the council; and the Malaeluans believed him to be a courageous man. But, standing there alone and exposed to Faleasa's challenge and the scrutiny of Malaelua, with his grey hair gleaming in the waking light, he looked utterly vulnerable. The row of blinds burst open again, and his wife knelt beside him and began to weep and plead with Faleasa. Tapu grabbed her by the shoulders, lifted her up, and flung her back into the fale.

As Tapu straightened up the shotgun thundered again. The large hunk of coral near his feet burst into tiny fragments.

Don't make me do it! Faleasa kept saying to himself as he reloaded the shotgun. Give in, please! Don't make me kill you! His whole body shook as he raised the shotgun to his shoulder and aimed it at Tapu's belly. One! Two! Three! Suddenly, at the end of the wavering gun barrel, he sighted Tapu sagging slowly to his knees. Almost crying with relief, he lowered the shotgun to his side, turned, and marched towards his fale.

The crowd parted to let him through, with Felefele trailing him, weeping. 'I had to do it,' he said when they entered their fale. She nodded.

At the council meeting that afternoon Tapu apologised to Faleasa; and in a brief speech Faleasa forgave Tapu and his aiga. (Later, when they tried to be friends again, they found they couldn't.)

As Faleasa left the meeting he glanced up at the sky and, as he recreated in his mind the flight of the dazzling gogo he had watched a few days before, he hummed to himself.

No one in Malaelua would ever again doubt his courage, and he would never again have to defend his mother's honour—she was dead.

Chapter 8

Except for Osovae, who knew otherwise, all the Malaeluan men believed that Lemigao was too ugly to win any woman, and they joked about it behind his back. Some of them even encouraged Osovae, who was by then married, to try to arrange a wife for his unfortunate friend.

Consequently, when the most sought after daughter of a leading matai confessed to her aiga that she was pregnant by Lemigao, her aiga and other Malaeluans at first refused to believe her. But, when her father in a raging cross-examination forced out of her a detailed description of her seduction and the ensuing affair, which had lasted for nearly a year, the unbelievable became less unbelievable and Lemigao assumed the image of a heartless seducer. The father and his threatening pack of male relatives confronted him but he politely denied everything—he even maintained that God was his witness. When they refused to believe him he countered their threats with more savage threats and with his bushknife, and—because they knew that he never backed down in a fight—they chose to believe him. A week later another young woman and her parents from the next village came looking for Lemigao, and the aiga of the Malaeluan girl realised he had lied. They rushed to his fale 'to hang and gut him', as the incensed father put it. But Lemigao's grandparents told them they didn't know where their ungrateful, fatherless grandson had gone.

Lemigao wasn't seen in Malaelua for about six months. In his absence the skeleton of his secret life surfaced bone by bone. The principal bones would never surface, however, because they were now the wives of important men, and confessions would ruin reputations and result in wifeslaughter. Not that Lemigao's conquests had been very numerous; but they had been passionately intense and secret and they had lasted until he ended them. He had delighted in seducing the daughter of one of the most pretentious matai in Malaelua, one or two arrogant women who had considered themselves above him and had joked about his burden, the spoilt niece of the Malaeluan storekeeper who had refused him credit, and three or four women (he could never remember the number) he had been infatuated with, ranging from a middle-aged wife who had been in American Samoa and had returned with what Lemigao believed to be alluring papalagi ways to a girl who was the pastor's prize student.

Before Lemigao's return the parents of the girl, who was now visibly heavy with child, sent her to live with relatives in Savai'i. The morning after he returned, some of the girl's brothers stood in front of his fale and challenged him to a fight. He got his bushknife and was on his way out to face them but Osovae and his father stopped him. When his challengers still threatened to attack him Osovae's father ordered them to leave, and they did so because no Malaeluan ever disobeyed him.

After this episode all parents became wary of Lemigao and everyone had to reassess their standards of male attractiveness to women. Until then Malaeluans had been intolerant of any type of deformity, and Lemigao, so everyone had agreed, was the most deformed creature in their midst. Now they had to accept that deformities such as Lemigao's crooked leg were attractive and even beautiful to some women.

As was the custom, a man could take a woman and live with her as his wife without being formally married in either the church or the registry office. Lemigao did just this with four women. The first one he acquired from a nearby village where he had gone to a funeral with his grandparents. She was a childless widow much older than he was. After a year of frequent quarrels, which were usually settled by his violently decisive fists, he sent her back to her aiga.

He appeared with the second woman a couple of months later. She was delicate and frail and gave out an utterly vulnerable silence, which made Malaeluans agree that Lemigao would destroy her quickly. On the contrary he was devoted to her and told all his friends that he didn't deserve such a good person as his wife. To Osovae he said that she was the only honestly religious and Christian person he knew; there wasn't a vain or dishonest bone in her body; and she loved him as he was. This idyllic episode, which he later branded as illusion and self-love, lasted for nearly two years. One morning he packed all the woman's possessions into a basket, stopped a bus, pushed her into it, and as it moved off waved cheerfully to her. To Osovae's stunned surprise Lemigao told him that his wife wasn't coming back: they had decided to part because it was a sin for a good person like her to live in sinful darkness with him. Didn't he love her any more, Osovae asked. Hadn't he told him before that there was no such emotion as love, protested Lemigao.

The third and fourth women were brief affairs. One lasted for six months before he took her into Apia and returned without her. The other lasted only a week.

As far as anyone knew none of these four affairs resulted in children, and one day Osovae told Lemigao that the Malaeluans were whispering that he, the 'handsome' cripple, now couldn't sire children. An enraged Lemigao first threatened to pulverise whoever was maligning him and then said that there were no children because he didn't deserve children yet. He hadn't known his father; his grandparents and his uncles and aunts had merely tolerated him because they thought he was a disgrace to their aiga; his mother had abandoned him to that fate when she eloped with another man soon after he was born. Gradually through the years he had earned his grandparents' grudging respect but, as for his other relatives, they were just a pile of excrement who were now too scared of him to bother him. His lone battle for survival in a hostile Malaelua had turned him into a completely selfish being who didn't deserve children. And he wasn't going to have children just to prove his virility to a herd of stupidly vain people.

When Osovae argued that all men wanted children, especially sons, Lemigao shook his head sadly and walked away.

After that Lemigao did not have another 'arrangement' for

a long time. Not that he abstained from women altogether—occasionally the urge became unbearable and he found release in a casual relationship. Then, in 1949, just before Easter, he brought Mua to Malaelua.

Mua was younger than Lemigao by about ten years; she came from a village near Apia. He met her at the Apia market where he had gone to sell taro. She was selling vegetables. When he started courting her she dismissed him, saying that his one good leg wouldn't be able to carry two of them very far. He retorted that his one bad leg alone could lift her right off the ground. She laughed and said she was solid and his bad leg looked too weak for her solidity. For nearly two days—she went home for the night but he slept at the market—this banter continued, until they had sold their crops. Then she finally agreed to be his wife. (He even promised to marry her in church but she said that she was too old and worn out for that.)

Before Mua agreed to marry Lemigao she explained that she had been associated with a series of tragic deaths and that she believed she brought bad luck to anyone who came close to her. She described these deaths briefly.

When she was about ten she had gone on a trip to Savai'i with her parents. On their way back a sudden squall erupted and the crowded ferry capsized; both her parents were drowned. An uncle, her father's youngest brother, brought her up and was good to her but he too died in an accident. While clearing bush he severed the veins of his foot with his axe and bled to death before he could reach the village. She was then about fifteen. Her mother's sister took her to live with her aiga. Like her uncle, her aunt was kind and generous and insisted she should attend the village school even though she was much older than the other children. It was there that she learnt to read and write. When she was about twenty her aunt fell ill and none of the healers could cure her. She died in the Apia hospital—the papalagi doctors said it was from an incurable disease called cancer. Not long after her aunt's death she married the son of a matai in her aunt's village. For nine years they were happy together; he was respected for his fishing skills; she was admired by the elders of his aiga because she was obedient and hard-working; they always had enough food and money; and the only sadness in their marriage was their lack of children. Although brewing and drinking faamafu was illegal her husband went drinking with some friends one night. When they were drunk his friends joked about his childlessness. A violent fight broke out and he was killed. As she had no children to tie her to his aiga, after some months she decided to accept another man's offer to be his wife. They shifted to live with his aiga in a village just outside Apia where he worked as a labourer. Life was hard because her husband's wages were low and there was little land to grow food on, but for four years she was content. Then her husband was imprisoned for six months for stealing some timber from his employers. When he was released the doctors found he had tuberculosis. He was in hospital for nearly a year; he died slowly.

Since his death she had stayed with his aiga, had contributed to their upkeep by growing and selling vegetables, and had refused many offers of marriage.

It was, she said, as if she had willed the deaths of all the people she had loved most dearly. But a moment later, her eyes twinkling with mischief, she told Lemigao that perhaps she wouldn't be able to bring bad luck to a cripple. He had always wanted to make Death his wife, Lemigao replied. They laughed for a long time.

Just before they caught the bus to Malaelua Mua said that it was fortunate she had no children to burden him with. 'I'm used to burdens,' chuckled Lemigao. 'Will you be able to bear my lifelong burden?' And he lifted up his club-foot.

'God has built me short and solid and low to the earth,' Mua answered, 'so I can bear any sort and shape and size and colour of burden.' They laughed about that too.

Most Malaeluans agreed, as soon as they got to know her, that she would be Lemigao's permanent wife. If he didn't marry her he was insane they told one another. She inspired a quiet confidence and trust, a feeling of permanence which made them feel clean and capable of overcoming their most hidden fears. Within a month she was established in Malaelua as if she had always been one of them, and when Lemigao told the Malaeluans about her previous life they refused to believe that she was the bearer of ill-fortune. It was all superstition, Faleasa declared.

That Christmas one of Lemigao's married cousins gave birth to a boy, and she and her husband let Lemigao and Mua adopt him. He, Lemigao, had agreed to the adoption, Lemigao told Faleasa, not because he now believed he deserved children but because children deserved to have wonderful mothers like Mua.

They called the boy Mose, after Moses in the Bible. They were determined to give him the best education they could afford. The New Zealand Administration was sending selected students to study in New Zealand on government scholarships, and Lemigao boasted to Faleasa that his son would some day be one of those students. Up to that time Lemigao had cultivated only enough land to satisfy his aiga's daily food needs; he had also kept a few pigs and chickens and cut and dried and sold copra and cacao whenever they needed money. Now, because of their son, Mua and Lemigao worked harder on their plantation and sold their surplus crops at the town market; they also sold more copra and cacao. They discovered, however, that the more money they earned the more money their relatives expected them to spend on aiga affairs, and there was little left to set aside for Mose's education. One day Lemigao mentioned his problem to Faleasa who took him into the Apia post office and opened a savings account for him. As they left the building Lemigao asked if Faleasa was positive his money was safe in there. Faleasa laughed.

Lemigao got Mua to look after their savings account, claiming that she was far better at figures than he was. So whenever they sold anything Mua deposited most of the money in their account. Lemigao always slept with their bank book under his pillow.

Malaeluans expected everyone to be generous. A good person was one who had limitless alofa and shared everything he owned. A mean person was the next worst person to a coward. Thus, when they learnt that Lemigao and Mua were saving most of their money—something which only papalagi and selfish Malaeluans did, and thank goodness they were few and far between—they gossiped about it. Lemigao's relatives accused them of being mean. 'It's the fault of that Mua,' they claimed. However Lemigao's and Mua's alofa increased abundantly as their plantation increased in size, and these accusations ceased. True, his relatives, told one another, Lemigao and his wife, like papalagi, saved some of their money, but they were generous with the rest.

Osovae's aiga was the first in Malaelua to construct a main fale with a concrete paepae and a corrugated iron roof instead of thatching. Many other aiga soon followed suit. But, except for the pastor, Lemigao was the first person to build a dwelling which resembled a papalagi house; he built it the year his son turned six and started school. It was a small single-room structure with a high concrete floor, a set of double windows at each side, a large front door and a back door, a corrugated iron roof without a ceiling, one wooden bed with a dirt-stained kapok mattress on it, two wooden chairs and a rickety table which Mua had bought at a sale in Apia, and a badly chipped tallboy with a long mirror on it. The house was situated a short distance behind their aiga's main fale which Lemigao persuaded his grandparents not to pull down. They had wanted him to build a large papalagi-styled house on the paepae of the main fale, but he told them he wasn't rich and foolish enough to satisfy their inflated hunger for status. However, humble though his house was, it gave evidence that Lemigao's aiga, the Aiga Laaumatua, once the poorest in Malaelua, was now worthy of consideration in the status scale.

Within a few years of starting school, Mose—with his parents' total devotion to making sure that he was the best pupil in Malaelua—was being lauded as a model son by his teachers, the pastor, and the elders. By the time he finished primary school all the other parents envied his parents for possessing such a handsome son who excelled in everything. As one elder said: 'Ugly Crooked-leg has produced the true Samoan son, who is fearless, obedient, and conscientious, and who serves his aiga with unquestioning loyalty and devotion.' However, the more the elders praised Mose the more friends of his own age he lost. Not that he appeared to mind: he seemed almost entirely self-sufficient, needing only his father's companionship.

Lemigao taught Mose to be a skilled fisherman, cultivator, and boxer. He was, Lemigao taught him also, not to be afraid of anyone or anything; he was to be well versed in oratory and the genealogies and in the history of Malaelua. In return, as Mose mastered reading, writing, and arithmetic he taught his father these skills. Children had nothing to teach their parents, most Malaeluans believed, and Lemigao was the first Malaeluan parent to allow his son to teach him anything publicly.

Mua's entire existence revolved round Lemigao and Mose: she bolstered their confidence when they needed it and bore much of every sorrow that came to them. Years later, an old man describing the relationship between Lemigao, Mua, and Mose claimed that Mua was the abundance and strength of the earth itself, the material out of which true myth was spun.

Mose was the first Malaeluan youth to pass the entrance examination to Samoa College, the principal government high school, which was in Apia. By that time his parents had saved more than enough money to pay for him to board.

It was in mid-October, during the last term of Mose's second year at boarding school, that a bus from Apia stopped in front of Lemigao's house and a student from Samoa College dismounted and hurried over to it. Lemigao would never forget how the student's uniform glittered in the noon-day light as if he was on fire, or how the heat suddenly enveloped him, and he found it difficult to breathe, or how the sight of a lone canoe, black against the foam on the reef, made him feel an almost overwhelming fear that the physical universe had been sucked away into a terrible void and he was utterly alone.

Even before the student handed him the letter he knew what was in it. He invited the student into the house and got the women of his aiga to bring him something to eat. While he ate Lemigao fidgeted with the still unopened letter as if it was burning his hands. Mua entered, saw the letter, and, recognising the fear in Lemigao, took it from him, ripped it open, and read it in silence.

'He is ill,' was all she said. Before Lemigao could react she got a basket and started packing. Then she brought him a clean shirt and lavalava. He got up and dressed and she sent one of the girls out to wait for a bus.

During the two-hour bus trip they didn't speak; they were even too frightened to look at the student who was sitting across the aisle from them.

Just as the bus was turning into the depot beside the town market the student told them that Mose had been taken to the hospital the evening before. Lemigao was on the verge of asking if Mose's illness was serious but Mua touched his arm and he remained silent. It was as though they had agreed that, if they didn't reveal their fear to each other, their son would recover. Even when they reached the hospital and Mose's housemaster told them in a hushed voice that Mose was seriously ill, they said little, and they maintained their stoical silence as a nurse led them through the crowded ward. Lemigao would always remember the odour of disinfectant and urine.

Drawn curtains, hanging from steel bars, surrounded Mose's bed and cut it off from the rest of the ward, which was simply a large open fale. The nurse pushed one of the curtains aside and waited for them to go in, but they hesitated. Eventually Mua stepped forward and Lemigao followed her in.

They stood beside the bed gazing down at their son. He was covered with a sheet up to his neck. He appeared to be sleeping peacefully; his breathing was easy and there were no visible marks on him or medical contraptions around him to indicate that anything was wrong with him. Mua brought Lemigao a chair from the foot of the bed but he shook his head and remained standing, his left arm draped across the headboard of the bed, his hand dangling only a few inches above his son's face. So Mua sat down. For a long time they just gazed at their son's face as if the whole meaning to their lives was reflected there.

That evening, while they were laying out their sleeping mats on the floor beside Mose's bed, a nurse came and took them to see the doctor in a small office at the end of the ward. As they walked along the ward Lemigao sensed that all the nurses and patients were observing them as if some unbearable tragedy had befallen them already; he would never forget how their eyes flicked away from him in one quick darting movement when he looked at them.

They went into the office and discovered that the doctor was a papalagi—a short rotund man with thick spectacles which magnified his eyes and made them look like fish eyes. As the doctor spoke, telling them through the nurse not to be frightened of him, they felt less afraid. The doctor's mouth chopped his words out crisply. For a second he reminded Lemigao of a bird pecking at a worm that was stranded above ground after a heavy downpour. Even his hands pecked at the air as he talked, and the round bald spot in the middle of his head shone in the light. The nurse interpreted for the doctor. Had their son been ill before? Had he suffered any serious accidents? Had there been any cases of serious illness in either of their aiga? To each question Lemigao shook his head.

Then the doctor explained that as yet they didn't know what was wrong with Mose; it was as if he had fallen into a deep sleep out of which he refused to be wakened. However, after more tests they would, he was sure, diagnose Mose's illness. Modern medicine, he concluded, could perform wonders.

Each day while Mose slept—and this was how Lemigao thought of his son's illness—he was wheeled on a trolley to the surgery and examined, and each day Lemigao and Mua were told that the doctors were on the verge of a diagnosis. This went on for nearly a fortnight. During that time most of the other patients and nurses and visitors from Malaelua, of whom Faleasa and Felefele were the most frequent, would examine Mose's face and tell Lemigao and Mua that there seemed to be nothing wrong with him. One old man suggested that they should get a traditional healer of physical maladies to treat Mose. Traditional healing was frowned upon by the hospital, so the series of healers whom Lemigao obtained through Faleasa came late at night when everyone was asleep. These healers failed too; Mose continued to sleep. Lemigao and Mua maintained their silent bargain never to discuss Mose's illness, but every night, in the humming silence of the sleeping ward, they prayed to God to heal their son. Lemigao even confessed his sins in detail to God and prayed that, if they were the reason for God's punishing him, God should take his life but not his son's. Every Sunday afternoon the Malaelua pastor visited them and they prayed together. Then Lemigao sought the services of healers who were reputed to be able to cure supernatural maladies. These healers too he brought to the ward secretly at night. They too proved ineffective. By the time Lemigao realised this he had spent nearly all their savings on the healers.

At that stage the doctor suggested that Mose's illness was more of the mind than of the body. After the numerous tests, he explained, they had found nothing wrong with Mose physically; it was as if he was mortally afraid and feared to confront whatever he was afraid of. The doctor tactfully inquired if anyone in their aiga had ever suffered from mental illness. Lemigao admitted that he and Mua weren't Mose's real parents, but, as far as he knew, his natural parents were not ill in this way. The doctor then divulged that he had interviewed Mose's teachers and some of his school friends but he had been unable to find any causes of Mose's illness. However, according to Mose's teachers, he was the most outstanding village student they had ever had. Yes, everyone who knew Mose said the same thing, Lemigao interrupted the doctor, swallowing back the beginnings of tears. The doctor said that the night before Mose collapsed he had written an essay about his aiga and village. But no one knew where the essay was. Perhaps a clue to his illness lay in that essay.

Next morning Lemigao went to the college and got permission to search for the essay in his son's possessions in the dormitory. He wept silently as he worked, feeling as though he was examining every precious memory of his son, as

85

though he was dissecting every vein in his own heart and destiny, hunting for meaning to unclench the grip of death which he was caught in.

He didn't find the essay. But he found a page of a letter which Mose had written to him but had not sent. He read it three or four times, refolded it, and, on his slow way back to the hospital, he stopped on the Lelata bridge, methodically tore the letter into a handful of tiny pieces, and let the pieces flutter down to lie in a scatter of silver tears on the almost stationary water. He watched until the ponderous current took every silver tear out of his sight. He never told anyone about the letter.

Mose died two nights later.

Lemigao refused, even when Faleasa tried to persuade him, to give his son a traditional funeral. He also, though the pastor threatened him with God's holy wrath, refused his son a funeral service in church. There was only a brief burial service by the grave.

That evening Lemigao beat Mua with his fists. He wasn't angry; he was simply committing an act he had to commit. She knew this and accepted it as punishment she deserved. She didn't utter a sound as the exploding pain shocked her into a numb darkness. Faleasa came, lifted her up, and took her to his home where Felefele revived her and cleaned and bandaged her wounds. A few days later, when she was well enough, she left Malaelua for ever.

He had divorced Death, Lemigao said to Faleasa when he inadvertently mentioned Mua. And Mose had freed himself from the curse of his parents. Faleasa was puzzled by this statement but he didn't ask Lemigao to explain it.

Lemigao never again spoke of Mua and Mose. It was as if they had never existed.

And he never took another wife.

Chapter 9

The move against Sau and Vaelupa was executed at the height of the most abundant bread-fruit season Malaelua had enjoyed in a decade and just over a month after the new pastor, one of Laaumatua's cousins, had been installed. The sickly sweet stench of over-ripe bread-fruit, rotting under the trees and aswirl with clouds of fruit flies, invaded everything but no one seemed to mind. The abundance of food had brought contentment; there was no urgent need to plant more crops; most of the young people played cricket on the malae nearly every afternoon. The women's and men's cricket teams, the Moli Moto and the Ula Mosooi, played other village teams on Saturdays. There was also more leisure to devote to gossip, and the rumours and stories were more imaginative, more vividly elaborate, more downright devastating than usual because there was more time to weave them in. Contented idleness, Laaumatua once remarked to Faleasa, was the succulent mistress of creativity —more children and stories and songs were conceived during the bread-fruit season than at any other time.

Hence, when the rumour about Sau and a certain young girl, one of his own nieces, detached itself from the general rotting bread-fruit stench and titillated, as it were, the contented idleness of the Malaeluans, it quickly took on highly enriched odours and deviously monstrous (but captivating) shapes, which in turn divided and multiplied in the contented but by then blazing imaginations of the Malaeluans until they reached the infinite possibilities of true mythology.

At the first few council meetings and at Sunday toonai held at the pastor's house after the rumour started the matai studiously avoided talking of it. Sau, the council leader, dominated proceedings, as usual, like a god too high up in the pure sky for any rumour-mongering mortal to pull down. But a monster struggled to break free from this thick hide of pretence. Soon, throughout the village some women dared to describe the general shape of the monster: a certain old man, who occupied the most respected position of tuua in their Christian village, was secretly betraying their trust by committing the most unmentionable of sins. Others soon gave the monster ferocious eyes: incest was the name of the dreadful sin. Still others gave it horns: the victim was a helpless, innocent waif who had sought refuge in the satanic old man's home. Others gave it a mouth and fangs: that poor child—may God protect her—was with child. The most viciously courageous gave the monster daring speech: the name of that violator of purity was Sau.

Sau's aiga tried valiantly to capture the monster by spreading counter-rumours. None of the rumours was true, they claimed. They tried to kill, cook, and eat the monster by declaring in uncountable whispers that it had been created and unleashed by evil people who were envious of Sau's goodness, selflessness, power, generosity, godliness, and honesty. Then they tried to defecate it in the form of windy exhortations to all true Malaeluans to join them in rooting out these power-hungry disciples of Satan.

When some Malaeluans asked Sau's aiga to identify these disciples and explain why that poor innocent girl was visibly fat with child, some of them reacted angrily and fights erupted, thus forcing Sau to discuss the monster in the council.

At the first meeting Sau, who was still sure of his control, threatened to banish any Malaeluan, titled or untitled, who believed any of 'these foul rumours'. He didn't say what he meant by this phrase. Vaelupa, Sau's right arm, echoed his threat.

The monster refused to die, however, and the next meeting found Sau employing more subtle tactics. His large eyes swam in tears as he openly admitted that 'these foul rumours' were about him. In front of God and for the dignity of Malaelua, he then declared, there wasn't a strand of truth in any of them. He was too old anyway, he concluded his oration. The meaning of this last remark escaped the matai who were still conjugally able, so to speak.

Still the monster thrived, rampaging freely through the imaginations of young and old alike, so that Sau, who by then was really looking his age, dared the council to accuse him openly. When no one did so he claimed that this was overwhelming proof of his innocence. Vaelupa supported him again. But just before the meeting ended Moaula suggested that the only thing needed to dispel the rumours was for the girl to confess who had made her heavy, as it were. Sau (and Vaelupa) agreed to this readily. The new pastor, Laaumatua's cousin, was to be the girl's confessor.

The girl's confession, as conveyed by the pastor to Moaula and a group of matai, confirmed the truth of the monster. For a stunned few days the matai didn't know what to do. Some of them asked the pastor to question the girl again, but he couldn't do so because Sau's aiga had sent her to relatives in American Samoa. The girl's disappearance prodded Moaula into calling a council meeting without Sau.

Shortly after the meeting began it became clear that the matai, except for Vaelupa, were convinced of Sau's guilt. Vaelupa made another long declamatory plea on his benefactor's behalf. The others tolerated his verbosity; then Moaula ordered him to furnish solid proof of Sau's innocence.

'But we have only the pastor's word that Sau is guilty,' replied Vaelupa.

'Are you saying our Man of God is lying?' Moaula asked threateningly. 'Well, are you?' Defeated, Vaelupa bowed his head and picked at the ragged edge of his floormat.

At that critical moment Laaumatua came in, sat down opposite Moaula, and apologised for his lateness and for not having attended the other meetings held since the 'trouble' started. A tulafale of Moaula's aiga told him of the meeting's findings and of their indecision over pronouncing sentence on Sau. Laaumatua nodded to Moaula and he immediately outlined the proposed sentence. The others, again with Vaelupa abstaining, quickly agreed to it and told Vaelupa to convey the decision to Sau. (Apart from Laaumatua, no one else would remember who had nominated the unfortunate man.) Vaelupa wept as he pleaded with them not to give him so humiliating a task. Moaula consoled him by declaring that, as Sau had admonished them when File-moni was banished, it was always heart-breaking to condemn one's friends or relatives but one must place God and the well-being of Malaelua above all else. When Vaelupa protested again Moaula ordered him to choose between the council and Sau, his friend who had proved utterly unworthy of his matai status and of God and country.

Vaelupa chose the council and survival.

When Vaelupa told Sau of the council's decision he rushed to Laaumatua's fale and pleaded with him, insisting that he was innocent of the girl's charges. Laaumatua promised to try to reverse the council's decision but he didn't do so. Sau next turned to Faleasa, hoping to draw him out of his silent madness, but his woeful pleas failed to fish the lucidly sane Faleasa out of the gaunt madman who just sat, his blank eyes reflecting the darkness outside.

Sau was banished from Malaelua. His aiga was allowed to continue as part of the village but Laaumatua influenced the elders of the aiga to choose an extremely ineffectual man to replace Sau as their head.

The day after Sau and his wife left, Laaumatua and Faleasa met in Faleasa's plantation fale. After discussing their victory they agreed that Moaula still needed careful guidance before he would be fit to lead the council. Faleasa asked his friend to continue giving him that guidance.

Chapter 10

1

His morning meal was very late, and this wasn't the first time either. Felefele and the other women were in the kitchen fale preparing it but they seemed to be too busy gossiping. Alone in the main fale, he felt ineffectual, with his anger and his groaning belly, and because he was supposed to be insane he couldn't very well call to the women to hurry up and bring his meal. Realising this, he felt trapped and, feeling trapped, his anger increased. Picking up his ali, he hurled it out on to the paepae where it landed with a loud clatter. The women only glanced over at him and continued talking as if nothing unusual had happened. So he rolled up his sleeping mats and threw those out too. This time the women didn't even bother to look. He sat down and slapped the floor with his hands. They were deliberately neglecting him. His meals were being served later and later and the quality of the food was deteriorating. Previously his aiga had catered to his every wish and whim; now he was lucky if they paid attention to his tantrums, which lately he had deliberately induced in order to attract attention. Felefele now slept with their grandchildren, leaving him alone to their voluminous net and one whole side of the fale. His daughters, who had once jumped to his every command, now ignored him. His grandchildren were no longer afraid of him and played all over his fale as if he didn't exist: some of the brats would even imitate his vacant stare, and would dribble and posture and then burst out into cruel laughter.

No, his angry mind was playing tricks on him, he said to himself, trying to erase these disturbing thoughts. An old man's mind tended to be bitter, vindictive; his family still loved him, needed him, owed him a lot. But, as his hunger rumbled in his belly and no one hurried to bring him his meal, his mind dissected the truth more ruthlessly. Felefele no longer made sure his clothes were mended, washed, and ironed properly; neither razor blades nor a comb had been brought to him for at least two weeks, so his face was a stubbled ugly grey and his uncombed hair was knotted and tangled; after he ate they didn't bring basins of water for him to wash his hands and mouth; most intolerable of all was the deadly indifference in their eyes when they looked at him—it was as though he was a mindless, emotionless creature, who from a sense of duty they had to keep alive. This last thought had stabbed at the quick of his being a few days before when, while he was having his evening meal, his eldest daughter and her brood of children who were serving him had discussed him as if he wasn't there, criticising his appearance and giggling at his emaciated body. That night, lying in his mosquito net, he had felt an almost unbearable sense of betrayal and had almost wept.

He broke. from his thoughts when a couple of girls brought his food, placed it before him rudely, and left again without bothering even to look at him. Grabbing the foodmat, he tipped the food and plates out on to the paepae. The women in the kitchen fale just dismissed him with momentary glances. Well, if he behaved like that he wouldn't get any more food, one of his daughters called out. Arms folded, he sat staring at the women defiantly. No reaction from them. An hour later fatigue defeated his defiance and he lay down and tried to sleep away his hunger and anger, his humiliation and self-pity, but he found he couldn't because his accusing mind was gripping him between its fangs and refusing to let him evade the truth about his aiga's mounting indifference to him. By midday, with the rising heat and his rumbling, ringing hunger, he was suffering attacks of dizziness, so he sat up; but the fale began to rotate slowly around him. He tried to rise to his feet but his trembling legs collapsed from under him and he hit the floor and fainted.

He surfaced from a pool of blackness to the sound of thudding fists, slaps, and kicks and saw Moaula beating Solimanava at the other end of the fale. Her long hair was wrapped firmly round Moaula's left hand while his right fist pounded at her mercilessly and he kept shouting at her that she was his wife to do whatever he liked with and it was her duty to take care of his father properly. She sobbed and shrieked and asked for forgiveness. Finally he kicked upwards with his right foot into her abundant stomach and sent her sprawling out on to the paepae. Felefele and the other women converged on her, lifted her up, and carried her into the next fale, with Moaula shouting that if they ever mistreated his father again he would murder them all. His son still loved him, Faleasa thought.

That night his aiga treated him exceptionally well but he sensed that most of them, especially Solimanava, resented having to do so. Felefele came and slept beside him, but when he tested her affections by touching her she moved away. At dawn he woke Moaula and told him he wanted to talk to him.

As they walked along the deserted beach strewn with shredded coral he confessed to Moaula his most secret fears about their aiga and how they were treating him. Near the end of his confession he suddenly realised that Moaula wasn't listening to him with any genuine sympathy. He was nodding his head and clucking his tongue and sympathising with him verbally but it was all pretence. Moaula was playing the role of a condescending father trying patiently to listen to the unreasonable exaggerated whinings of a child. Like the rest of his aiga Moaula didn't need him any longer, but he still refused to believe that the freedom he thought he had won was only a trap from which he couldn't escape. Of course they still needed him and he would regain their respect, he told himself. All he had to do was to reveal that he was only pretending to be insane. And admit he had failed in his quest for personal freedom? He decided against any revelation.

In the following weeks his aiga's service was prompt, lavish, polite, and efficient, but the forced quality of it all hurt him intensely. His aiga were serving him, not out of any love for him, but because they were afraid of Moaula. At times, when he found it too difficult to evade this conclusion, he would wander through the plantation and allow the sight of lush growth to bandage his pain, or he would stroll to the western end of the village and, in the small palm grove overlooking the sea, sit at the edge of the cliffs and let the smell and sight and feel of the sea's mystery wash out his pain. He had set up a new leadership in Malaelua, had succeeded in becoming a free man, a new person who saw lucidly. But he had also made himself utterly unnecessary to his aiga. Perhaps true freedom was this very quality of not being needed even by those you loved? His quest was all self-love and vanity; he was still trapped in his own juices, odour, excrement; he was simply an old man nobody needed any more; he was valueless—that was the truth of the matter.

2

Sometimes, as he sat on the edge of the cliffs, he escaped into Malaelua's past which offered him lucid glimpses of the past and the present, and of the darkness that was the future.

One particular saga about the mythological hero, Pili, contained what Faleasa believed was the essence of prepapalagi Malaeluan beliefs about the cosmos and man's place in it, and it also offered him truths about his present reality.

At first Pili was known as Pili-Pau or Falling Lizard because, as a baby, he had fallen down to earth from the heavens in the form of a lizard (a creature which in prepapalagi days was worshipped by many aiga). Pili had been sired by the god Tagaloaalagi, the Supreme Creator, on a mortal woman, Sina—the daughter of Tavaetele, the alii of Malaelua—whom Tagaloaalagi had abducted.

A barren old woman who lived alone at the outskirts of Malaelua found Pili on the narrow peninsula just to the east of the village. Because he was an ugly, sickly lizard she nursed him secretly in her fale. As he grew, however, she found it difficult to keep him hidden. Every time she went out she ordered him not to leave the fale, saying that people would abduct him because he was so handsome. (She had been careful never to let him see his own reflection.)

One morning while she was away in her food garden Pili accidentally threw his ball out of the fale and chased after it. As he played with the ball he wandered further and further away from home and found himself on the banks of a spring. He was thirsty so he scooped up some water with his hands. When he saw the ugly creature reflected in the water cupped in his hands, he gasped, dropped the water, and fled home. The pools formed by the water he had dropped were called Loimata-o-Pili—Pili's Tears.

When the old woman returned Pili told her to gaze directly at him and to keep her eyes still. He stood in front of her, confronted his reflection snared in her eyes, and wept. The old woman, whom he loved as his mother, tried to ease his pain by telling him that he was a demi-god.

'Who are my real parents?' he asked. She told him but pleaded with him not to invade his father's kingdom in the Ninth Heaven as he would be killed. He ignored her warning and planned to beg his father to restore him to human form. Sina, his mother, wouldn't help him in his quest, the old woman told him, for she loved Tagaloaalagi. 'I have other allies,' Pili replied. Because he had been forbidden to associate with people he had befriended three spirits who lived near his home. They were Tausamitele—Insatiable Appetite, Lelemalosi—Strong Flight, and Pouliuli—Darkness. It was with these friends that he devised his plans.

When all was ready Pili and the other two spirits clung on to Lelemalosi and he flew with them to the Ninth Heaven. Tagaloaalagi's home was a gigantic fale surrounded by sharp spears and guarded by two ferocious giants standing at each post of the front entrance. Being a lizard, however, it was easy for Pili to sneak into the fale through a gap in the blinds. He surveyed the interior and found a secret exit at its northern end.

That night, while Tagaloaalagi snored beside his wife, Pili stole in, picked up his sleeping mother, and carried her out through the secret exit to his waiting friends. They hid her in a nearby cave and sealed the entrance so that if she woke she would think it was still night and go back to sleep. Then they returned to Tagaloaalagi's fale; there Pili's three companions hid and he sat down directly in front of the fale.

The sun rose and the giants saw him. They rushed to capture him but Pili said, 'I have kidnapped your mistress and will kill her if your master doesn't agree to meet me.' The giants woke their master who stormed out to confront Pili, but Pili immediately said that he was his son. Tagaloaalagi told Pili that he had cast him into the form of a lizard because Sina, his mother, had committed adultery with another god. And now he would kill him once and for all. 'If I am killed Sina will be killed in revenge,' said Pili. 'But, if you set me three tasks and I perform them successfully will you lift the curse off me? In return I will restore Sina to you.'

That night Tagaloaalagi set Pili his first task. He was to eat a mountain of fish which the giants had caught that day. When Tagaloaalagi and his giants woke the next morning they gnashed their teeth angrily because the fish were gone. They didn't know that Pili's friend Tausamitele had eaten them.

That afternoon Pili had to attempt his second task. This was to race the giants down a river which was alive with treacherous rapids, whirlpools, and waterfalls. As soon as they all dived into the water Pili disappeared. But when his opponents reached the still pool at the bottom of the last waterfall Pili was already there, drying his long hair in the sun. Once again Tagaloaalagi and his servants gnashed their teeth in frustrated anger. Unknown to them, Lelemalosi had picked Pili up and, made invisible by Pouliuli's darkness which surrounded them, he had flown Pili to the end of the course.

That evening, in the light of the blazing fire that always illumined the front entrance of the fale, Tagaloaalagi told Pili that he was to watch what his giants were about to do, and for his third task he must try to imitate it. The giants rolled themselves into balls with their feet in their mouths and then, within seconds, swallowed their bodies up to their necks. Pili laughed haughtily. 'Watch!' he called to Tagaloaalagi, and he jumped into the air and vanished completely but continued to talk. He had of course simply leapt up into Pouliuli's huge mouth.

Before making himself visible again Pili reminded Tagaloaalagi that Sina would be killed if he didn't keep his word and restore him to human form. Tagaloaalagi promised again, and as soon as Pili was visible turned him into a handsome youth who from that time on was known as Pilimanaia, Pili the Beautiful.

Tagaloaalagi then demanded his wife back, but Pili said that Tagaloaalagi must first give him a live ember, a fishing-net, and a war club—possessions which mortals did not then have. Tagaloaalagi shook his head furiously. Pili turned to leave. 'Surely you won't kill your own mother will you?' Tagaloaalagi called. Pili smiled and said, 'Wait and see.' Tagaloaalagi rushed into his fale and was soon back with the gifts that Pili had demanded.

According to Malaeluans, this was how mortals acquired these three wonderful possessions. Pili taught the Malaeluans how to use fire and fishing-nets. With Tagaloaalagi's war club he conquered the whole of Samoa and unified it for the first time. He also taught his people how to cultivate crops and use kava. And he forged links between Samoa and other countries such as Fiji and Tonga.

During Pili's reign—and he was just, benevolent, and generous—the country enjoyed a long period of peace. He had three sons and a daughter. When he grew old, he decided to divide his kingdom among them, believing that his children would live together in peace. At first they did so but then war broke out between them. He tried to persuade them to make peace but they ignored him. His only daughter, his favourite, even called him a useless old man who had no right to be alive.

That same night Pili vanished from Malaelua. Some Malaeluans claimed that he had jumped up and been swallowed by his friend Pouliuli and would refuse to become visible again.

After examining some of the meanings of the saga, and the possibilities were infinite, Faleasa concluded that, like Pili in his bitter old age, he too had voluntarily jumped up, as it were, into a living death, into the living darkness of Pouliuli. This conclusion did not frighten him: it was consoling, like being suspended in the core of a timeless sea, without a beginning or an end; and all was well.

3

One afternoon, while Faleasa was lying in the low under-growth of the palm grove, with a cool breeze rippling like feathers over him, his eyes closed against the harsh light of the sky, the incessant hum of mosquitoes and the sea's throb hovering at the rim of his hearing, an old man detached him-self, like a flower unfolding, from the wilderness of his childhood memories. For a moment he tried to shut the old man out, fearful that the dead once unleashed would haunt him with their stench, their decaying shrouds, and their accusations, but he found that he didn't really want to resist the old man. Let Lazarus rise, he thought.

Late one afternoon, while Osovae and some of his friends were playing hopscotch on the road, Lemigao rushed over and told them there was a strange-looking old man sitting on the church steps. They ran across and found a crowd of children at the bottom of the steps gazing silently up at the scrawny figure seated on the topmost step. The old man was wearing only a tattered lavalava that barely covered the middle part of his body; his hair was fluffed up in a tangle of silver white; and even at that distance Osovae could see that his skin was wrinkled like the bark of an ancient mango tree. Sitting there cross-legged, his arms folded across his chest, his cold eyes staring unwaveringly down at them, the old man looked as if he had emerged from the very fabric of the church itself to claim ownership, and no one was ever going to shift him.

Suddenly the old man unfolded himself and got to his feet as though he was struggling to stand up in a thick liquid. At that, most of the children retreated a few paces. Extending his sticklike arms towards the sky, with his fingers like threatening claws, the old man threw back his head, gazed into the fierce light, and opened his mouth as if he was screaming in terrifying soundless pain. He maintained this posture in absolute stillness until Osovae had counted to twenty. Then he began to advance down the steps. The children scattered, and Osovae found himself hiding with Lemigao in the clump of bread-fruit trees only a short distance from the church.

As they watched, the old man stopped on the bottom step, shielded his eyes with his right hand, looked east, then north, then west, then south (which was to the steps behind him), shook his head slowly, as if he hadn't found what he had been looking for, threw his head back again, and hurled another long soundless scream into the sky's belly. He froze in that position for an even longer time than before, the air seeming to prop him up.

'Why doesn't he do something else?' Lemigao whispered impatiently to Osovae, and before Osovae could stop him he hobbled out of their shelter, stood directly in front of the old man (but at a safe distance), and called, 'Hey, old man, wake up!' The old man maintained his motionless position. So Lemigao advanced to within ten yards of him and yelled, 'Hey, madman, wake up!' Only the rise and fall of the old man's chest revealed that he was alive.

Osovae went and stood beside Lemigao, and the other children followed. No one spoke as they scrutinised the old man. His wretchedly emaciated body was covered with the dark scars of healed sores and boils, on his arms and legs ugly open sores wept with pus, his rheumy eyes were embedded in their sunken sockets, his teeth were rotting in the gums, his skin was ingrained with dirt, and he stank as if he hadn't washed for a long time. One of the boys started laughing and pointing at the old man's genitals which were exposed through a tear in his lavalava. Osovae ordered the boy to shut his rude mouth.

Running off, the boy poked his tongue out at Osovae and then chanted, 'Osovae likes madmen! Osovae likes madmen!'

Just as Osovae and Lemigao turned to chase him, the old man groaned loudly and buckled to the ground, where he lay writhing and groaning and grasping his belly. The other children fled to the main road and watched from there while

Osovae and Lemigao looked helplessly at the old man and at each other. Then Osovae said he would get his father and ran off as fast as he could.

Osovae's father and two other men of their aiga picked the old man up and carried him towards their fale, with Osovae and Lemigao and the other children trailing them. When they reached the fale Osovae told the children that the old man was still alive, and they dispersed.

The fale's blinds were drawn, and some of the women of Osovae's aiga bathed the old man, bandaged his sores with herbs, rubbed coconut oil into his skin, dressed him in a clean lavalava and shirt, curtained off one side of the fale for him to sleep in, spread out some sleeping mats and pillows, laid him down, and covered him with a blanket because he was shivering. Osovae's father then got the most skilful healer in Malaelua to treat him. The healer massaged him until warmth spread through his body again and he regained consciousness. Osovae's eldest aunt propped him up on the pillows and fed him some hot fish stew and tea. Osovae slipped in behind the curtain and sat down by his aunt. The old man reminded him of a helpless baby and he wasn't afraid of him any more.

That night Osovae dreamt the old man was his father but, unlike his real father, the old man allowed him to behave like a child, encouraged him to cry openly when he felt like it, and talked to him when he wanted to talk. The dream ended with the old man picking him up gently and—laughing until the whole earth and sky and sea were alive with his joy—releasing him up into air as soft as feathers, where he floated, wheeled, swam, and turned cartwheels in limitless, endless freedom.

The next morning Osovae and the other children were told not to disturb the old man's slumber. When Osovae demurred his mother hurried him out of the fale. After their morning meal Osovae's father ordered him to go to their plantation with two of his cousins to get some firewood and foodstuffs and make an umu so that their important guest— and his father stressed this phrase—would have something good to eat when he awoke. He also sent some men fishing.

On the way to the plantation Osovae wondered why his father was treating the old man in this very special way. He couldn't think of any good reasons for his father's behaviour but it pleased him.

That afternoon Osovae eagerly volunteered to help the women serve his father and the old man their meal. Their guest stepped shyly from behind the curtain, sat down opposite Osovae's father, and the two men started to talk as if they had always known each other. (Nothing was said about the old man's fit of insanity the previous afternoon.) Osovae noticed that their guest looked much younger now that his hair had been trimmed and combed and his beard shaven and clean clothes hid his scarred body. The mad, startled look had gone from his eyes; and the memory blossomed in Osovae's mind of the dazzling monarch butterfly he had studied the week before as it freed itself from its cocoon. This memory would become more vividly real as Osovae came to know the old man better, and his father later said of the old man that fragile beauty had been born out of the crucible of madness and suffering.

Osovae was astounded by their guest's appetite. For a time he couldn't believe it was possible for such a small thin person to eat so much, but their guest, while maintaining a freely flowing conversation, devoured—but his manners were impeccable—innumerable helpings of fried corned beef, baked taro and luau, and four mugs of cocoa, and finished by crunching his way through a heap of cabin bread thick with coconut jam.

Osovae sensed that his father and the other elders felt honoured and humbled by the old man's presence. This surprised him because his father rarely felt humble before any other person. The old man had brought with him a contagious feeling of generous goodwill which Osovae had rarely seen between the elders of his aiga, and especially between his parents.

Immediately after washing his hands and mouth their guest said that he was still tired and needed to rest again.

While the old man slept everyone gathered in the next fale and Osovae's father impressed upon them that their guest was never to be left alone during the day. If he went out someone must accompany him. Only at night was he to be left alone; then no one was to follow him, even if he wandered off into the darkness. The old man was to be their guest for as long as he wanted to stay, and everyone, *absolutely* everyone, was to treat him with limitless alofa; they were extremely fortunate to have him as a guest—it was a blessing from God on their aiga. All this puzzled Osovae still further but he knew better than to ask his father to explain: his father never offered explanations to children or women. To Osovae's surprise his father chose him to be the old man's companion and told him that the old man would teach him much.

The old man slept all that afternoon and night. In the morning Osovae woke before anyone else and found a light mist of rain swirling round outside. He quietly picked his way across the fale and peered through the curtain. The old man wasn't in his net; only his blanket lay there like a skin which he had shed. Frightened that his father would punish him for not accompanying their guest now that it was day, Osovae hitched on his working lavalava and started to run through the village in search of the old man. Soon he was soaked but he didn't notice the cold. Most aiga were still asleep; the blinds of their fale were down and shivered in the rain; there was nobody about. He grew frantic when he couldn't find the old man. Besides his fear of being punished by his father he also felt a huge weight of loneliness as though someone precious had deserted him. He tried to swallow his tears as he ran home, his feet pounding into the pulpy sand, his breath coming in ragged gasps, the mist of rain weaving round him like a natal shroud he was trying to discard.

The sound of a hymn from the direction of his home broke through the humming of the rain, and he ran faster, frightened to the depths of his bowels that his father would have discovered his failure by now and be waiting to give him a beating. Suddenly, through a gap in the fale blinds, framed there like hope, he saw the old man, sitting in front of the curtain, leading the morning lotu, and his fears vanished.

While he was helping his mother serve his father and their guest their morning meal, the old man asked him to come and share his food. It was impolite for children to eat with guests so Osovae glanced at his father. He nodded. With bowed head, Osovae sat down beside the old man, who ruffled his hair and told him to eat, eat, the food was delicious. Osovae looked up and the old man winked at him. As Osovae started to eat, the question eased into his thoughts: Would he miss his parents as deeply as he had missed the old man while he searched for him that morning? Remembered, but then tried to obliterate the memory that, after his most recent beating from his father, he had wished his father would die.

Soon after the meal the old man and Osovae were left alone in the fale. For a long time, as the old man stared out into the rain, he picked at his teeth with a piece of palmfrond rib which Osovae had got for him, using a corner of his lavalava to wipe the rib clean every time he withdrew it from his mouth. Osovae watched the old man and the rain and felt both beings were of the same sleepy harmony that was droning in his head. Unexpectedly the old man flicked his toothpick out on to the paepae and asked Osovae if he could read. Osovae nodded. The old man said that he was illiterate, completely without education, and that he would like Osovae to read aloud to him from the Bible.

Osovae got the Bible from the wooden trunk in which their most precious belongings were kept, sat down opposite his companion, and started reading from Genesis; but the old man wanted to hear the passage from Ecclesiastes that prophesies the end of the world. As Osovae read it the old man listened with his eyes closed. Every time Osovae faltered in his reading his listener corrected him, and Osovae concluded with mounting admiration that the old man must know that particular passage by heart. He became sure of this when he read the last few verses: the old man, with his eyes still shut, the veins in his eyelids blue and twitching, recited the verses aloud, his bass voice vibrant with power, the words tumbling off his tongue in a silver stream of music.

For over an hour, until the rain had been sucked away by

the dark ground, Osovae read all the passages the old man requested, and enjoyed doing so. After every passage the old man sighed deeply and said that he wished he was literate, but when Osovae couldn't pronounce certain words the old man pronounced them for him and at times even recited whole passages. At the end of the readings the old man opened his eyes, congratulated his young reader on his literacy, and said that one day when he had the time he too would learn how to read and write and to add figures. He then spat a thick gob of phlegm out of the fale, wiped his mouth with the back of his hand, blinked repeatedly, and explained that he was merely an ignorant creature with an insatiable memory that wouldn't leave him alone. Did Osovae know that his type of memory could devour a person bit by bit, bone by bone? Osovae nodded, even though he didn't understand; he sensed that his companion was speaking more to himself than to him. Suddenly the old man seemed to remember Osovae and, breaking out of himself with a dazzling smile, asked him if he believed there were people in the world who remembered in exact detail everything that had happened to them—every sight, taste, smell, thought, and, worst of all, every pain; such people were the most tortured of God's creatures. Osovae realised that the old man wanted to be rescued from his thoughts, so he said that his father insisted on the importance of training one's memory because it was a gift from God. The old man sighed and agreed with him but maintained also that literate people were lucky because they could store, describe, imprison, exorcise, and identify their memories in written form—the printed word was their escape from the ravenous, rapacious, fearless appetite of memory. The old man paused briefly and then asked if Osovae had understood what he had said. Osovae nodded his head out of politeness and the old man explained that the papalagi missionaries, by bringing the magic of the written word to Samoa, had rescued their people from the brutal nightmare swamp in which their collective memory was rooted and from which it derived its ferocity; had turned their people's attention from the irrational madness of their vain and violent blood to the humane light of the word. This was a crucial mystery Osovae should contemplate when he grew up: because he was literate he would have no difficulty in unravelling it. As for himself, he was now too old and too illiterate to think this mystery through to the light. And, because Osovae possessed the magic of the written word, he had nothing to fear from his cannibal memory. Noticing that the rain had stopped, the old man chuckled, tweaked Osovae's chin, and assured him that some day he would understand everything that he had tried to explain.

That afternoon, while they were walking over the slippery track towards their aiga's plantation, which the old man wanted to visit, he suddenly stopped and, turning to Osovae, asked: 'But how much longer will the word be able to contain, describe, and exorcise the horror being born out of the world's collective memory? How much time is left before the light is sucked up by the bleeding ground and the air without the word drives us into silence?' Weeping soundlessly, the old man began to shuffle up the track again, with Osovae following and not knowing how to console him.

The first three circles of pebbles appeared on the second morning of the old man's stay. The circle of about two feet in diameter on the grass in front of the church was composed of small round pebbles, obviously taken from the paepae of a fale. The two boys who discovered it counted twenty pebbles. At the centre of the circle was a larger pebble that looked as though it had been oiled with coconut oil. The boys got their father to look at it; and their father, a staunch deacon, dismissed with an impatient shush-sh their whispered claim that an aitu had made the circle at midnight. He collected the pebbles, took them to their fale, and scattered them over the paepae. The second circle, an exact replica of the first one, was found above the pool by the first woman to go there the next morning. The pattern held her interest momentarily; then she decided it was the work of a child and brushed it off the bank into the water with her foot. The third circle was located immediately before the main entrance to the school, and the head teacher's young daughter who found it collected the pebbles to use as knucklebones. That day no one discerned any connection between the three circles, not even when the pastor's wife, while cleaning the church pulpit that afternoon, discovered that the embroidered pulpit cloth was missing; or when the communally owned bucket, which everyone used to draw water out of the pool, had disappeared; or when the head teacher couldn't find his only pair of scissors.

However, when three more circles were found the next morning—one in front of the pastor's house, one in front of the store, and one in front of the largest fale bordering the malae—and it was discovered that one item of property (of little value) had been taken from each of these homes, the Malaeluans concluded that the circles were a joke, a prank. The more superstitious, which meant nearly all Malaeluans, nevertheless started whispering to the effect that the circles and petty thefts were the work of aitu. When the oldest matriarch, who was respected and feared for her ability to cure ailments believed to be caused by the supernatural, argued vehemently that the circles were omens of doom, the whispering transformed itself into alarm and dread. The most respected elder, a shrivelled remnant from the first half of the previous century, tried to calm their fears by arguing that, if it was the work of an aitu, it was harmless, playful work and the circles were payment for the worthless items taken. Perhaps it was a joke being played on them by a *boy* aitu then, one brave matai suggested.

When more circles appeared the next morning and caused vividly horrible rumours of destruction to scuttle through the village, Osovae's father summoned a council meeting and also instructed the pastor to preach against the existence of aitu and to label belief in them as heresy. The action failed to suffocate the rumours of doom. Men in every aiga stayed up all that night but they saw no one, at least no being with visible human form. The next morning, to their desperate amazement, three more circles were found in front of three other homes, from each of which one item had been stolen.

The old man insisted on playing suipi every afternoon and

he always let Osovae win. On this particular afternoon, while they were playing at the side of the fale where the old man slept, Osovae glanced up at the fale dome and down at his cards again, refusing to believe what he had seen. Then, while the old man was involved in considering his next move, Osovae forced himself to look up again. Lodged in the thatching just above the heads of the posts were many of the missing items. For the remainder of their card game he didn't look up at them again, convinced that if he didn't see them they would vanish, and if they vanished his friend wouldn't be branded a thief or an evil aitu. During the next hour or so after their game the old man talked, but Osovae couldn't concentrate on what he was saying, and as soon as the old man said he was going to rest for a while he wandered out of the fale, trying to devise ways of protecting his friend from the wrath of Malaelua. By evening he had decided to tell his father the truth: his decision being determined by his earlier observation that his father wanted no harm of any kind to befall their guest. When he told his father he laughed and promised that the old man would not be harmed.

Early the next day Osovae's father called another council meeting, this time at the pastor's house, and told the matai that *their* guest was responsible for the circles and thefts, but no one, absolutely no one, was to discourage the old man from staying. Osovae's father emphasised that their humble village was extremely fortunate to receive a visit from the old man. 'Anyway aren't the circles of pebbles enough payment?' he concluded. The other matai laughed and readily agreed to his request that, if their guest was ever seen entering any fale or making his circles at night, they were to pretend they couldn't see him. When Osovae's father got home after the meeting he again stressed to Osovae the vital importance of not following the old man at night.

From that day on the Malaeluans competed to allow their guest to steal things from their homes; they also forbade the deliberate destruction of the circles.

At night, when Osovae didn't have to be with the old man, he sometimes met Lemigao and described to him in elaborate detail what he and the old man had done that day; but he couldn't explain to Lemigao the meaning of the old man's monologues, only that he sensed the old man had suffered as no man had suffered before, and that he was full of alofa, understanding, and wisdom. 'But the old man's nuts!' Lemigao, who was jealous of Osovae's role, retorted one night. Osovae wheeled and left him standing there. A little later Lemigao was hobbling along beside him, apologising for his cruel remark.

Another night Lemigao asked Osovae if he knew where the old man was from. Osovae had to admit that he didn't and that when he had asked the old man he had talked about something else. 'You must find out,' Lemigao insisted. So Osovae tried again. This time the old man said that a person was what he was, and what that person had been in the past was of little importance. Anyway one's past was a black abyss into which one was too afraid to fall, he added. When Osovae told Lemigao that the old man hadn't divulged anything of his past, Lemigao argued that the old man didn't want to do so because he had probably been a criminal, a murderer even. Osovae immediately threatened to end their friendship. Lemigao apologised and then suggested that perhaps Osovae's father knew the old man's history. Osovae reluctantly asked his father and had to confess to Lemigao at their next meeting that his father had refused to tell him anything. (Once again he had had to suppress his guilty wish for his father to die.) Lemigao then suggested that he should ask his mother but Osovae confessed that his mother had little time for him. That night, when he tried to sleep, he sensed that his time with the old man was coming to an end but he persuaded himself he would be able to accept it: he hadn't needed anyone's love before, not even his parents', so why should he need a sick old man to comfort him!

It was Sunday night, thirteen days after the old man had come. A quarter moon hung like a curved blade over the heads of the palms bordering the fale. Everything outside was the colour of melted lead, and under the trees, rooted into the sinews of the sleeping ground, shadows crouched and breathed and waited. When Osovae saw the old man slip out from behind the curtain and walk silently over the paepae and towards the beach he rolled out of his net and picked his way out of the fale.

The shivering came from the pit of his belly and out to all the cells of his body as silence and the eerie light enveloped him, and he nearly ran back into the fale. He didn't need anyone! He strengthened his resolve, and when he was able to control his shivering he crept into the darkness under the nearest clump of banana trees and waited there, knowing what the old man was going to do.

'He's gone! He's gone!' he cried, to wake up his aiga as daylight filled the fale. He pulled aside the curtain and revealed a roll of sleeping mats, a neatly folded mosquito net, all the clothes they had given the old man, and a thatching bare of its stolen inhabitants.

His father scrambled up as if he was struggling to breathe, rushed over, and examined everything. He kept asking everyone if they knew where *his* guest had gone. Osovae watched him. No one offered his father consolation, so he ran out of the fale, stopped on the edge of the paepae, yelled back to his aiga to get up and search for his guest, and then rushed down towards the centre of the village.

When Osovae was alone he sat down and gazed into the emptiness which the old man had once filled. He could hear people coming out of the neighbouring fale and joining in the futile search.

His mother was the first to return from the search and to find the circle of pebbles in front of their fale. Soon a large crowd was gathered round it. Osovae went out, pushed his way through the silent crowd, and, standing beside his mother, looked down at the circle. The centre pebble was missing. Tears began to stream down his face and he gazed up at his mother but she looked away. He felt a warm hand on his shoulder but, recognising it as his father's, he shrugged it off, crouched down quickly, scooped up the pebbles, and started to stumble through the crowd, clutching the pebbles to his chest.

'Let me help you!' his father called, but all he heard was the sobbing of his whole being and the rip and tear of his heart shedding its caul of innocence.

Innumerable stories about the old man circulated in Malaelua after his disappearance. The most believable ones described him as the son of an unmarried woman who had been the servant of a childless English missionary couple. His mother had died giving birth to him and he was adopted by the missionary and his wife. They reared him and taught him Samoan and English, and, when he revealed a gift for languages, German also. (At that time Germans were the most numerous foreigners in Samoa.) As the only son of influential missionaries and the most gifted student at the main LMS school he was destined to be the first Samoan sent abroad to be trained for the ministry.

In England his teachers were impressed by his intelligence, his diligence, and his knowledge of languages, and they predicted a brilliant future for him. During his vacations he toured all over Europe, especially in Germany. After three years in England he requested to be allowed to continue his theological studies in Germany. Even though his parents thought the Germans were barbarians they granted his wish.

He was away from Samoa for nearly ten years. When he returned, all Samoans were very proud of him: he, they boasted, was proof that Samoans were capable of acquiring the new knowledge.

For nearly three years he worked with his parents to consolidate the LMS faith; then, after Easter in the third year, he moved out of the mission compound to live with his Samoan relatives. (It was rumoured that he had quarrelled with his parents.) He refused to attend church for a few months but eventually did so when his mother fell ill. She died slowly of a mysterious illness that ate away her energy and flesh and bone. His father died of the same disease soon after her. No one noticed that he had not let any doctor examine his parents.

For a short time he continued his religious activities. Then he started to appear publicly in a strange uniform which the LMS's rivals, the Catholic priests, identified as a German military uniform. Soon afterwards he refused to speak any other language but German and took to organising military parades with his students at the theological college. His superiors who, because of his actions, were by then the brunt of cruel jokes, asked him to leave. He accused them and his dead parents of having stolen his soul and replaced it with the crippled soul of a papalagi, and then stormed out of the mission forever. The LMS missionaries told their congregations that he was insane, and the people believed them because they thought that the human brain was capable of containing only so much learning: an overdose would burst it.

As he drifted from village to village the people started calling him 'the German'. However, derision gave way to awe when stories spread that he could cure all kinds of mysterious illnesses. When more stories told that aiga and villages which treated him kindly always harvested rewards after he left, the people came to believe that God was working through his madness to cure the incurable and to reward those people who were kind to the unfortunate. Everywhere he went they welcomed him and encouraged him to stay.

Some people noticed one feature of his activities: whenever he helped others he succeeded, but whenever he tried to do something for himself he failed and the state of his mind deteriorated further. For instance, many witnesses claimed that he had fallen in love with a kind generous widow—the widow had died a horrible death, blood bursting mysteriously from all her pores. Others said that he had once vowed he would stay in one particular village for the rest of his life, but a famine had struck the village, and to save the people he had moved out.

Some people also noticed that he was sane at times but that his sane spells soon ended, as if he didn't want them to last. Some argued that madness was his escape from his suffering.

He kept claiming that he was illiterate, and whenever anyone mentioned his parents and his education in Europe he denied them. From the time he left the mission he never again spoke English or German—at least not in public. As he moved through the villages his ability in Samoan became respected by even the most famous orators. He was trying to find his true soul, he would tell his hosts, but when they asked him to explain further he would talk of something else.

Over the years the belief that he was in his own unique way a messenger of God, living proof of God's ability to suffer the world's pain, became firmly rooted among the people, and no one dared mistreat him for fear of God's wrath. One story told of a village which drove him out and soon after suffered an influenza epidemic which killed nearly all its inhabitants.

After he disappeared from Malaelua the Malaeluans agreed that he had left voluntarily and therefore nothing dreadful would befall them. Osovae didn't tell anyone that he had caused the old man's departure.

You swim up out of the painful depths of memory to feel again the agonising prison of your ancient carcass around you like Lazarus's foul bandages. You betrayed the old man.

You see him return from the beach, and stop in front of the fale, kneel down and, with short pecking movements, place each pebble of the circle. In the light he seems a shadow which is trying to attain definite life and form and identity but which is still part of the night's gloom, still more vapour and darkness than flesh. You see yourself, the fourteen-year-old boy, divorce yourself from the darkness in which you have been hiding, as if you too want to become flesh, and walk towards the old man. He doesn't see you until you are standing in front of him in the shadow he is casting over the circle. Then he is gasping, shielding his eyes with his hands, and rising to his feet. 'Go away! Go away!' he cries. But you refuse to leave; you have caught him before he can complete the circle which, by containing his madness, gives meaning to it. He tries desperately to complete the circle; he looks away from you; he kneels down again, his whole body shaking violently, his right hand clutching the final pebble and scuttling round on the sand like a blind crab, groping for the centre, the sanctuary. But you reach forward and wrench the pebble out of his hand. He stifles a scream, wraps his arms round his body, and weeps soundlessly. You watch the boy arch back his arm and, before you can stop him, he throws the pebble, the heart, into the darkness. You don't hear it fall. Suddenly there is a silence as deep as the vault in which you have buried your guilt all these years. Before you the old man stands like a withered tree, arms and fingers outstretched to the moon's blade, his head thrown back, his mouth uttering that soundless scream, unable to bear the world's pain any longer. You retreat from him, wheel, and escape back into the safety of your bed.

You suddenly remember that you betrayed him in 1914, the year the First World War erupted, and you understand for the first time the old man's prophetic question: How much longer will the word be able to contain, describe, and exorcise the horror being born out of the world's collective memory? And then you remember the Second World War and you understand his final question also: How much time is left before the light is sucked up by the bleeding ground and the air without the word drives us into silence? During all your comfortable life, isolated in your tiny islands, in your safe village, in your cocoon of power, you have never really experienced the depths of terror or understood the bestiality that was born (and is still being born) out of what the old man described as our vain and violent blood, out of the brutal nightmare swamp in which our collective memory is rooted and from which it derives its ferocity.

As the light of understanding continues to illumine your memories you admit to yourself that you loved him, that you betrayed him in the fatal moment you denied that love: a love which your father and mother denied you and which all your married life you have denied your wife and children.

'Vanity, all is vanity' you hear the old man reciting from the Bible. Your bid for freedom in these last years of your life is vanity too, you now tell yourself. Where then is the escape, the meaning to your life? In madness or silence like the old man? But you shrink from that final irrevocable decision because your carcass, aged and tired and painful though it is, still hungers to breathe a little longer.

Chapter 11

Faleasa couldn't stop the memories from flooding into his heart in an endless stream of accusing pain, and the more his pain deepened the more he was forced to confront his past.

To his demanding father, who had awed him with a limitless fear (the aptest description of how he had really felt about his father), the son had been merely an extension of himself, further proof of his virility, to be shaped in his own image in order to continue his brand of leadership— and his name of course. His son's individuality was ignored, and at times when he had tried feebly to assert it his father had treated this slight assertiveness as a disease which must be cured even if it meant using violent intimidation. He was, he realised now, to *be* his father, which meant to be afraid of nothing and nobody (at least, publicly); to be arrogant, autocratic, and bigoted; unquestioned ruler of their aiga; a bully and tyrant who enjoyed other people's fear of him. And he had been proud of his father and of the insufferable little bully he had become under his father's tutelage. He had even enjoyed his enslavement to his father. As he pondered further he understood more clearly why people enjoy being enslaved, why they willingly sacrifice their freedom, their true selves, their individuality: life was immeasurably easier if one became a castrated pet.

All his life he had been afraid to think objectively about his father. Now he had to, so that through understanding him better he might learn to forgive him, might change his fear of him into love.

The strongest impression everyone had had of his father was of bigness, though he was quite short and lean of muscle, sinew tightly wrapped round a frail frame. But the feel of everything about him was of bigness, even the slow way he smiled. This feeling emerged because nothing about him had been spontaneous; everything had been deliberate, coldly calculated and executed: every idiosyncrasy, every move was well rehearsed, even his apparently spontaneous outbursts of fearful anger. 'You must have full control over everything, especially over yourself', he remembered his father saying. 'Without control you will never be a true leader; others with better, more ruthless control will control you.'

When Osovae (as he was then) was born his father was thirty years old, and he lived to be sixty-five, but to Osovae his father had never seemed to age. Because his father was so deliberate about everything, his mannerisms and the way he walked and talked and laughed hadn't aged with his body. Even the way he died was deliberate.

'A man is only truly dead when all that he leaves behind him—the fruit of his flesh and hands and mind—are no longer remembered,' his father said as they sat beside the lamp, his father cradling their aiga Bible in his lap. (The rest of their aiga were asleep in the mosquito nets that filled the fale.) It was a chilly night and they had their sleeping sheets wrapped round them. Only when they were alone would his father emerge from his cocoon of cold aloofness and confide in him, but here again his father's confidences were usually confined to exhortations to him to lead without needing anybody else. Nevertheless he treasured those brief moments because they were the only times his father permitted him not to be the son who in public had to live up to his father's almost unattainable standards of how a leader should behave.

He was thirty-five years old and had five children. As his father resumed his reading from the Bible and he scrutinised him surreptitiously, he concluded that his father had never treated him as a child. As soon as he was able to talk his father had treated him as a man, with all the ideal traits of a man, the most valued of which were indomitable courage, infinite patience, a limitless capacity to tolerate pain without a whimper, and the ability to hide one's true feelings behind an impregnable mask of controlled aloofness. According to his father, a true man had control, and it didn't matter if that man was five years old or a hundred; and any son of his was a man superior in all the masculine virtues to all other men. One of these virtues, however, his father forbade him: that of being what his father called 'licentious'. Licentiousness, his father claimed, was the worst sin any true man could commit, despite the well-known fact that he had sired three illegitimate children and was still, at the age of sixty-five, having secret affairs.

As his father read, his voice picking methodically at the shadows which shivered at the light's edge outside, he sensed that something was amiss, and for a long puzzled moment he couldn't identify it, only that it had something to do with his father. He tried not to think about it, but every time he glanced at the shadows fear clutched at him. He noticed that his father stopped reading and was gazing at him. 'Do you want to ask me something?' his father said. It was more a plea than a question. He shook his head even though he did want to. 'Are you sure?' his father said. Again he shook his head, afraid that, if he did ask, his father would interpret it as weakness, proof that he wasn't yet a true leader and hence above all the emotions common to weaker beings. His father gazed at the floor, his shoulders trembling. A few minutes later, when his father looked up, the mask of inscrutability was there again. 'You must never let your children or anyone else see you are weak,' his father said. He wondered what his father had been sad about. 'My father, Manutagi, was a weak man, so weak that though he could have got the Faleasa title he was too scared to try. Manutagi was afraid of other men so he remained a taulealea to the miserable day he died.'

His father then explained that Manutagi had wasted his life, had been a good-for-nothing weakling who had even allowed two other men to elope with his two wives. 'One of these women was my mother,' his father added. 'I never knew her and it was good I didn't. She must have been a slave to the weaknesses of her flesh. Manutagi—and I am still ashamed of my father's memory—became a joke in Malaelua: parents held him up to their children as an example of who not to become. He lived off the Aiga Faleasa all his life and died of a stroke brought on by obesity. I was fortunate. An uncle took care of me, gave me an education at the pastor's school, and showed me what a man should be. To that uncle I shall always be grateful.'

'But Manutagi, your father, must have possessed some worthwhile quality?' he heard himself ask.

'If one can call suffering a good quality, then there was something worthwhile about him,' his father answered. Paused again.

A few unbelievable moments later his father emerged from his secret depths and talked vividly of his father Manutagi as though it was vital for his own son to inherit that memory and not be able to forget it.

Manutagi, his father said, was a small man, light-boned and frail, a build which throughout much of his life he conveniently used to justify his many illnesses and his cowardice. He was ugly also, with a head much too large for his body, protuding ears, which made the children call him Lapiti—Rabbit, an overly flat nose, thick lips, and ebony skin, which made the women call him Meauli— Negro, small eyes that never looked at you directly but darted slyly around you, feeling out your weaknesses, and short bandy legs pockmarked with weeping sores, which made the young men call him Kaupoe—Cowboy. (His ugliness he also used as justification for his cowardice.) He never spoke unless he was spoken to; and his speech was always almost inaudible, mumbled, and extremely polite, as though he was afraid his words would offend even the air.

That was how he had been in the second half of his life. In the first half, the period before his first wife ran off with another man, he had been quite optimistic, jovial, self-assured, confident—and considered handsome by some women. He had a thriving taro plantation which he had hacked out of the bush. The Aiga Faleasa respected him for his hard work and loyal service; and he was as courageous as any normal male. But, after his wife—a young buxom girl who needed more satisfying than Manutagi could give her—left him, he started to neglect everything, especially his physical appearance, and to cultivate imaginary illnesses in order to justify his disintegration as a man, his downward transformation into a coward. To try to help him, the then Faleasa, an uncle, arranged another wife for him, a middle-aged widow from a neighbouring village.

This woman, who was a calculating shrew, speeded his disintegration. From the morning she entered his fale to the night she disappeared from it, leaving their only child to him, she nagged him into a self-imposed deafness, into greater self-effacement, into stuttering speech, into neglecting his appearance further, into uncontrollable secret bouts of. weeping at night, and into more imaginary illnesses. The Aiga Faleasa thought he would improve after she was gone. He didn't. His baby son became his new excuse for disintegrating further; his inability to procure another wife to take care of his son made matters worse; and, when he heard that his relatives couldn't persuade any other woman to be his wife, he sought his final self-destruction in food. When he had handed his son over to a married sister and her husband to bring up, he himself moved from relative to relative. They didn't mind. They felt sorry for him and gave him all the food he craved. He ate and ate.

'I hated and despised him,' Osovae's father said. 'As I watched him deliberately suffering I told myself that a man who could accept all that punishment and demand more was either insane or utterly fearless.' He stopped without saying which his father had been, so Osovae asked him. His father looked up; there were tears in his eyes. 'I never had the courage to decide what my father was. It was far easier to label him a coward.' Paused. 'You've got to decide whether I've been a good or bad father for our aiga and village.' Another pause, with his father looking away into the darkness. 'It doesn't matter to me how you judge me because I am to die soon, but it's important to you and how you're going to live out the rest of your life.' Then his father straightened up and said rather impatiently: 'There is nothing more to say. I *know* you will choose my way, the way of strength and godliness!'

As Osovae lay beside his wife that night he remembered

his father telling him that he was to die soon. He couldn't get rid of that memory; it was as if his father had purposely embedded it in his mind, the same way he had deliberately planted Manutagi's mythology and choice in the cells of his being.

On a wet afternoon seven days later, when they were returning from their plantation, his father asked if he was ready to lead their aiga. He nodded. 'Good,' his father said.

Three mornings after that his father stayed in bed. He told their aiga he had a fever but would be all right in a day or two.

He died that evening, not long after their lotu, which he had conducted as always.

Now, as Faleasa thought about it, he admitted that he hadn't felt sad at all when his father died; indeed, he had felt as though a fist in which he was imprisoned had un-clenched to set him free.

He picked at the memories, encouraging them to bleed.

His father had arranged even his marriage, he now admitted to himself.

Felefele was the only daughter of the highest-ranking alii in the next village. Osovae didn't know of her existence until his father one day mentioned her name, traced her aiga's genealogy, and added that she was well known for her 'charm, purity, and devoutness', a girl any worthy son would marry. The hint escaped Osovae because at the time he was having an immensely enjoyable affair with a Malaeluan woman and had no intention of marrying anyone. A few days later, his father told him that everyone praised Felefele as a perfect young lady, worthy of her father who was a godly aristocrat. Osovae continued to pretend that he didn't know what his father was driving at, but his father, while they were planting taro one morning, told him it was time he got married. Osovae remained silent, hoping his father would interpret his silence as disagreement. But his father assumed the opposite and announced that he and his leading tulafale would visit Felefele's aiga the following week and arrange the marriage.

At that time most Malaeluan marriages were common

law ones: if a couple wanted to live together as a man and wife they simply eloped and did so. But Osovae and Felefele were to marry in church. As the status-conscious heir he had become, Osovae, observing the elaborate marriage preparations, soon forgot that he didn't want to marry yet and convinced himself that marriage to the daughter of an important alii was the proper thing for a man of his rank, and that marriage in church to a religious, conscientious, obedient virgin was the dream of every aristocratic, properly brought up son.

The marriage ceremony and feast were the most lavish that Malaeluans had ever witnessed, marvelled at, and participated wholeheartedly in. The Aiga Faleasa slaughtered almost the whole of its large herd of pigs and flocks of chickens; all the Malaelua taulelea went on a fishing expedition and returned with an abundant catch of fish, crabs, and lobsters; the women fished for sea and shellfish on the reefs; mounds of taro and yams were baked in giant umu; three months before the feast a special pit was dug, a smoking fire was lit in it, and numerous bunches of bananas were put in to ripen underground in the smoke; long rows of temporary shelters were erected on the malae to hold the feast in; hundreds of guests and relatives came from all over the country, bringing more food and ietoga and money and other wedding gifts. The Aiga Faleasa, everyone agreed after the wedding, were genuine aristocrats, uncorrupted practitioners of the true faa-Samoa in their generosity, their display of wealth, their behaviour, and their hospitality.

Osovae was unable to deflower the virginal Felefele for at least a week because he found to his agony that she didn't arouse him physically. She was the least attractive of all the women he had tried to make love to, and because she was inexperienced she didn't know how to arouse him. She simply lay with an arm over her face, which only made matters worse. Another handicap was the fact that they slept in the main fale with most of his aiga.

None of the women he had desired before had ever refused him, and he had never failed them; consequently he had believed that his sexual prowess was exceptional. Hence when he failed with Felefele he blamed her.

One Saturday morning, after another frustrating night of trying, he went with her into their plantation on the pretext of getting foodstuffs for their aiga's Sunday umu. Once hidden in a clump of trees he instructed her to use her mouth on him. She shook her head. He ordered her again. While she worked at him he closed his eyes and deliberately thought of the other women he had enjoyed. When he was erect he pushed her down on to her back.

While he was using her he realised that she was enjoying it all—the humiliation, the pain and the bleeding, his stabbing flesh—and, on realising this, he discovered that his need for her was greater, more binding, than his need for any other women he had known. ('Real power is when you can dominate and use others', he remembered his father saying.)

He had enjoyed violating her; she had enjoyed being violated. During their life together she had used this mutual feeling to control him and keep him away from other women.

As Faleasa thought of his parents he wept, knowing that he too had been born out of violence: his father, he was sure now, had destroyed his mother. 'Only the powerful have the right to survive'—his father's voice rang in his head.

Chapter 12

Faleasa and Laaumatua sat talking in the shade of the palm grove. It was late afternoon and a brisk wind was weaving in from the sea, bringing with it the familiar smell of coral, as high tide punched at the foot of the cliffs in an endless swirling smother of waves. Nearly three months had passed since Sau's banishment.

'Is anything the matter?' Laaumatua asked. Faleasa shook his head. 'You don't look well. Everything still all right at home?' Looking away, Faleasa nodded. 'That's good. But you still don't look very well,' Laaumatua said.

'I'm all right I tell you!' Faleasa snapped.

They were silent for a minute or two, then Faleasa apologised for getting angry, but Laaumatua laughed and said that short-temperedness was the God-given privilege of old men like themselves. Mosquitoes continued to hum round them and they waved them away periodically with small branches which they had ripped off nearby shrubs. Occasionally a dry coconut thudded to the ground somewhere behind them in the grove.

'Our member of parliament is visiting us tomorrow, Laaumatua said. 'Several days ago a messenger brought me a letter from him. Elections are only a few months away.

'You don't sound pleased about his coming,' said Faleasa.

'He may query the new leadership we've established.'

'He won't. I made him our MP. He'll support us.' Faleasa paused and then added, 'He's a good man as well.' But even as he said this he felt hypocritical, knowing that Malaga, his cousin and their MP, had visited them only once since the last election; and he suddenly started to resent Malaga for his car and fleet of trucks and spacious papalagi house, and for the status and power and the comfortable life he was enjoying in the capital—luxuries which he, Faleasa Osovae, had got for him by ensuring his re-election every three years for the past nine years. He refused, however, to admit to himself that Malaga had used him (and was still using him). Malaga Puta was the alii of the third most powerful aiga in Malaelua. At Faleasa's insistence, nine years earlier, Malaga had been elected to parliament unopposed. Two other matai had sought the nomination but Faleasa had manipulated the matai council into persuading them not to stand. Since then Malaga had been unopposed.

'I suppose he's coming to ask us to return him again. Not that I think we shouldn't,' Laaumatua said.

'Is there any other matai who's more suitable?' Faleasa demanded, annoyed at his friend for making him question to himself his faith in his political choice.

Laaumatua pondered for a moment and then said, 'What about Moaula?'

'He's too young and too rash and he's had very little education. Malaga is still the best educated man our district has produced.' He went on to remind Laaumatua that Malaga had been the first Malaeluan to go up to form two in the Apia government school; that he had worked in New Zealand for ten years, attended night school there, and mastered the use of figures and English; and that he also understood modern government.

'There are rumours,' Laaumatua said.

'What rumours?' asked Faleasa. Laaumatua said he didn't want to talk about them if it would anger him further. 'I'm not angry!' insisted Faleasa.

So Laaumatua divulged that, according to some rumours emanating from Apia, their MP, who was a very powerful figure in the government, being chairman of three of the most influential government boards and committees, was in financial difficulties and was illegally using government funds and accepting bribes. He was also involved with women and drinking to excess. 'Do you want to hear the rest?' Laaumatua asked. Faleasa nodded. 'Some of our people who are living in New Zealand have written to their aiga saying Malaga's life there wasn't an exemplary one.'

'Go on,' Faleasa prompted.

'Malaga never attended that night school he's always talking about. He doesn't have the educational qualifications he claims he has. He spent most of his time living off a series of women.' Paused. And then said emphatically, 'And he was deported back here. Yes, *deported* back.'

Stunned, yet unwilling to believe Laaumatua, Faleasa struggled to protest. 'Can't be true!' he finally managed to say. 'Can't be!' It was impossible for him to have chosen Malaga, to have put all his faith into the Malaga whom Laaumatua had just described, impossible for Malaga to have used him all these years.

'Why don't you ask him tomorrow?' suggested Laaumatua—then, remembering that Faleasa was supposed to be insane—'If you like, Moaula and I can do it?'

Faleasa shook his head and said, 'I'll come to the meeting and find out for myself. If he's pretending to be what he isn't I'll know.'

Just before they returned to the village Laaumatua picked up a stone, brushed the dirt off it, scrutinised the veins in it for a moment, and then lobbed it out over the edge of the cliff. It curved up and out and then plunged down, continuing to curve in towards the cliff-face, and was quickly lost from view. As he turned away from the cliff edge Faleasa saw in his mind the waves reaching up in one huge mouth and swallowing the stone. 'The rumours aren't true!' he insisted.

'I hope not,' Laaumatua replied.

As Faleasa had expected, the fale and houses of Malaga's aiga, where the meeting was being held, were packed with all the matai from Malaelua and the neighbouring villages which constituted Malaga's electorate. In the kitchen fale Malaga's aiga and a horde of Malaeluans were cooking pigs and other food for their guests. On the paepae of the main fale, in full view for the people to envy and be impressed by, were stacks of bread, barrels of salted beef, cartons of tinned fish and cabin bread, and sacks of sugar and flour. As was the practice this was Malaga's momoli to his voters, visible and expensive proof of his gratitude to them for having elected him to parliament—and of course visible generosity to help persuade them to give him another three-year term. Parked beside this fale under the shade of some bread-fruit trees stood Malaga's new pickup and a large truck, one of his fleet of trucks.

Faleasa shuffled up the paepae through the aisle between the stacks of foodstuffs. The matai occupying the front fale posts moved aside to let him in. As he walked towards Malaga they all tried not to look too closely at him. He was again the venerable old man gone mad. Malaga, for an unguarded moment, looked frightened of him and then the fright melted into his usual beaming smile and he patted the mat beside him, indicating that Faleasa should sit there. Faleasa sat down and continued to stare vacantly at the mat in front of him while Malaga greeted him with the customary oratory and then told the other matai, especially Moaula and Laaumatua, that he was particularly grieved that his *father* (meaning Faleasa) was ill. As he continued in this vein he put his left arm round Faleasa's shoulders. At this point, Faleasa observed, Moaula looked annoyed, almost ashamed, that he had come. Malaga, noticing that Faleasa didn't have a shirt on, stopped speaking, took off the new floral shirt he was wearing, and dressed Faleasa in it, like a concerned mother shielding her baby from the cold. The shirt smelt heavily of sweat and perfume and liquor. The matai from the other villages, following Malaga's lead, told Moaula that they were indeed sorry his illustrious father had been afflicted by this terrible disease; God would eventually heal him of course.

A few minutes later the kava ceremony to welcome Malaga formally to Malaelua began, and everyone stopped paying attention to Faleasa. Throughout the ceremony Faleasa concentrated on studying Malaga and, now that he was deliberately examining his cousin with some degree of objectivity, the first inevitable conclusion he reached was that nine years of comfort had turned Malaga into a soft ball of fat. His belly and the rolls of flab, which began with his breasts and flowed in waves round his waist, flopped

down over his belt; his small face looked lost in his large
jowls and numerous chins; a fine layer of sweat covered his
skin like dew; and his crew-cut hair added to the effect of
violent cunning which Faleasa hadn't observed in him
before. In an attempt to appear less fat Malaga was trying
to sit upright and hold in his stomach. When he laughed or
spoke, he did his best not to do so too heartily because this
caused his rolls of fat to wobble too conspicuously.
A pompously vain man, Faleasa concluded.

The kava was distributed cup by cup to the matai
according to their rank. Previously, as the highest alii,
Faleasa had always received the most important cup, but
not even Malaga suggested that he should still be accorded
this privilege, and Faleasa further concluded that he was no
longer of use to Malaga, that he no longer existed for the
gathering; and his pain grew more intense because even his
own son hadn't insisted he should be given his kava cup.

After the kava ceremony the leading tulafale, a member of
the Aiga Faleasa, welcomed Malaga with an elaborately
ornate speech. Malaga replied with his usual loud oratory
which, Faleasa noticed for the first time, was a crude
mixture of colloquial speech, inappropriate proverbs and
sayings, and superficial and inadequately reasoned out
ideas, delivered in an over-confident manner. When Malaga
finished his speech he took out his wallet and, using one of
the youngest matai, distributed lafo to every matai except
Faleasa, the largest amount, as was the custom, going to the
tulafale who had spoken.

Malaia, Malaga's wife, who, Faleasa noticed, was now
almost as large as her husband, brought six large bottles of
whisky and placed them in front of Malaga. She didn't even
bother to greet Faleasa as she had always done in the past.
Liquor was prohibited in the district, and Faleasa waited to
see what Malaga was going to do with the whisky, such large
bottles of which were a luxury rarely seen in Malaelua.
Malaga declared that the whisky was 'medicine' for those
matai who needed it badly. The matai laughed. Faleasa
noticed that most of them were eyeing the bottles, hoping to
be given one, and he couldn't believe that for nine years he

had been bought—yes, bought was the only word for it—by Malaga with such crude offerings: money, food, false praise, and now whisky. A time-honoured custom had been turned into a mockery, a cheap system of buying; and he, Faleasa, had allowed it to happen. This realisation almost forced him to shout out in protest.

Moaula and Laaumatua, now the power-makers in Malaelua, were given a bottle of whisky each; the remaining bottles went to the four most influential matai from the other villages.

Malaga called to his aiga and they began serving the meal. Faleasa staggered up slowly. Malaga reached out to help him but Faleasa edged away and started to shuffle out of the fale.

Once home Faleasa had to fully accept the painful fact that for nine years he, and therefore all Malaelua, had been bought by an unscrupulous, dishonest rogue. Such a betrayal was made worse because Malaga was of his blood —blood did not betray blood, aiga did not sell aiga. By his blindness to Malaga's character, he, not Malaga, was responsible for having allowed the market system of the town to infiltrate Malaeluan life and taint its very centre with a deadly cynicism. How often in the past had he heard the other matai joking about selling their votes to the highest bidder but he had closed his mind to such cynicism. How Malaga must have secretly laughed at them for allowing themselves to be bought so cheaply. Suddenly he realised that he was wearing Malaga's shirt; he ripped it off and threw it out of the fale; but for a long time afterwards he still smelt Malaga on his skin. For the first time he noticed that all the surrounding fale and houses were empty and he knew that the people were hanging around Malaga's aiga, waiting for their share of Malaga's momoli, their price for abdicating control of their national destiny to a man who was using it to fatten himself.

It was time to start work in Apia when Faleasa got off the bus in front of the Savalalo market four days after Malaga's visit to Malaelua, picked his slow way through the crowded vegetable stalls to the stalls of cooked food at the back just above the sea, bought a breakfast of hot pancakes and a mug of tea, found a vacant place at one of the tables between the rows of stalls, and started to eat, dipping the first round pancake into the tea to soften it before he began chewing it. He had caught the first bus as dawn broke, and all his joints ached from the trip. Right now his aiga would be searching for him throughout Malaelua and when Felefele discovered that a few dollars were missing from her basket they would perhaps figure out that he had gone to Apia and would come looking for him. This thought amused him.

In recent years he had rarely visited Apia because he found the long bumpy bus ride too exhausting, but his visits had never failed to overwhelm him with awe and wonder and make him feel that he was just an ignorant villager who had no hope whatsoever of attaining the abundant promise of perpetual youth and sophistication, of modern wisdom and rich living which Apia seemed to offer. Now, as he ate and studied the crowds, heard their cacophonous sound and inhaled their smell of slow decay, felt the layer of damp grime like the slimy skin of stingray under his bare feet, and saw the ugly disfigurements on the bodies of buyers and sellers alike, knowing the bitter truth about Malaga as he did, a shiver of fright fingered painfully through him, and the pancakes and tea, which he always looked forward to on his town visits, turned tasteless in his mouth. Getting up, he pushed his way through the crowd to the main street, and once he was free of the market noticed that he was sweating heavily even though he didn't feel hot. The sky was overcast and a cool breeze was flowing up the street, sweeping the dust and debris before it. For a time he stood and gazed at the weaving traffic, which reminded him of a panicking school of mullet being hunted by barracuda. He could not dispel the dread feeling that for the first time in his life Apia was utterly hostile to him and wanted to shield Malaga from his threat.

He had to go through with it. So he started walking, more a slow deliberate gaining of footholds than a walk, along the footpath.

Malaga's new house, which Faleasa had visited twice before, was situated in the middle of Togafuafua, an area which extended from behind the massive Mulivai cathedral up to the foothills behind the town. Once it had been mainly swampland but over the years since the advent of the missionaries it had been reclaimed by the tenants who rented the land from the Catholic Mission. As Faleasa shuffled over the embankment that carried the main road through the neighbourhood, unable to escape the stench rising from the mud and stagnant water which choked the ditches beside the road, he coughed often and spat out the phlegm. On his previous visits the stench and the sight of the dirty overcrowded shacks and fale, spread like decaying teeth between the more opulent houses, had not upset him at all. Now they did. The whole smother of dwellings looked as if it had never been young, as if it had risen out of the depths of the swamp already old and ugly and diseased and would remain like that forever.

When he reached the driveway to Malaga's house, which was half hidden from view by a high hibiscus hedge, he paused for a moment and straightened his clothes.

Except for the white window-frames, white front door, and white roof, the two-storeyed house was the colour of the open sea, a deep blue which made it appear more massively squat, an anchor holding down Malaga's acre to the belly of the area which turned to mud and threatened to flow away every time there was heavy rain.

Faleasa stopped in the front doorway and looked in. Malaga's wife Malaia was asleep in the centre chair across the room, with her chin resting on her chest and her hands folded across her massive paunch. She filled the chair to overflowing. Snores escaped occasionally from her quivering mouth. Quietly Faleasa entered, sat down in the chair opposite to her, and watched her. A thin trickle of saliva was dribbling from the corner of her mouth. Buried in that ugly caricature, he thought, was the beautiful young nurse he had advised Malaga to marry twelve years before. A fly landed on her nose and started moving up towards the lump of congealed sleep in the corner of her left eye. When it reached its destination Malaia's eye blinked open, startled the insect away, and shut again.

Faleasa looked round the room. The walls and ceiling were painted with brown tapa designs, making the room seem smaller; one wall was covered with framed photographs, chiefly of Malaga in his youth and in New Zealand; most of the furniture was new and had chrome frames and plastic covers; a TV set stood against the wall behind Malaia; and four large bouquets of plastic flowers were dotted around on low tables. On his earlier visits Faleasa had marvelled at the expense and told himself that this was the style Samoans should pursue. Now the room overpowered him with its cluttered pretentiousness; there was no feeling of homeliness about it; like the windows of the large stores it had been set up as a permanent display to impress visitors. This was a confidence trick to hide the fact that Malaga was living beyond his means. This was power without conscience, symptom of the sickness in the nation's soul, a tragic mimicry, an absence of faith in things Samoan. Till now he had been blind to Apia and Malaga and Malaga's breed—fearful shadows in black ties and sunglasses. And, he thought, this is the empty glittering shadow of a life that many people, and especially the new leaders, are now striving for. The centre has held all right but the sickness has invaded that centre and is infecting it cell by cell.

He coughed. No reaction from Malaia. He coughed again. Her head jerked back; her lips opened and closed repeatedly; her eyes blinked open, and—as they focused slowly on him—widened with fright. She struggled to get out of her chair. He coughed again and she was free of her chair and scrambling out into the passageway where he heard her ringing Malaga and frantically telling him that *he* was there. Malaga must have asked who, because she said, 'It's the mad old man from Malaelua and you'd better come quickly.'

In a few minutes she was back in the room with two hefty women. When they sat down to face him he greeted them in the customary way. They just stared warily at him, so he asked if anything was the matter. Malaia shook her head and sweat dripped off her chin.

'I am *not* sick!' he said.

The women fidgeted. 'Malaga will be here shortly,' Malaia said. So he sat in silence and enjoyed their discomfort.

Before long the pickup truck scrunched up the driveway, screeched to a dust-coughing halt before the front door, and Malaga was out of it and puffing into the sitting room. Faleasa smiled broadly, as he had always done in the past, stood up, and shook Malaga's surprised hand.

Pretending nothing was amiss, Malaga told the women to get a meal for Faleasa, took the seat his wife had vacated, pulled a large white handkerchief out of his shirt pocket, and started to wipe the sweat from his face. 'Very hot, very hot!' he kept saying. 'Everything all right at Malaelua?'

Faleasa nodded. 'In case you think this person is still ill,' he said, 'let me tell you now that God has been kind and has healed this unworthy person.'

'We must give thanks to our Heavenly Father for healing my father!' Malaga replied, but Faleasa knew that his cousin was not convinced of his sanity.

'Yes, I am well again. And just in time too.'

Sitting up, Malaga asked, 'Is my father anticipating trouble in our village?'

'Nothing that I can't solve now that I am well again.' Faleasa paused; and then, emphasising each word, said, 'Nothing that I can't solve in order to ensure your re-election.' Malaga leant forward immediately, eagerly awaiting his explanation. Faleasa could smell his rapacious eagerness and for a moment it frightened him, but he explained that a faction, which he couldn't identify as yet, was plotting to unseat Malaga. However, he and Laaumatua and Moaula were protecting Malaga's interests, and this plot would come to nothing. When Malaga insisted on more information Faleasa promised to give it to him soon.

'Shall I visit Malaelua and help root out this plot?' Malaga asked.

Shaking his head, Faleasa said, 'No need to. Now that I am well again you will be re-elected. Have I ever failed you in the past?' Malaga shook his head. 'So leave it to me.

At no time are you to believe information about the Malaelua elections unless it comes from me or from Moaula or Laaumatua. You are not to believe even the matai of your aiga, as some of them might be involved in the plot. I will send Moaula to Apia regularly to keep you informed. In the meantime we have to operate in complete secrecy until I have identified the dissident faction and destroyed it. All you have to worry about is to visit Malaelua on election day and cast your vote.'

'Is there going to *be* a ballot?' Malaga asked.

'Not very likely; but, if we find that a ballot is the best way to bring our opponents into the open, then we'll have a ballot. It will show who voted for who. Get me?'

Malaga winked. 'Good! Good! Good!' he repeated, and then called to his wife, 'Food! Food for my father!'

Before leaving that afternoon Faleasa said, 'Our village still believes I am insane. This is a perfect disguise from which to observe what is happening.' Again Malaga winked, and they laughed together for a long time. Then Malaga took Faleasa to one of the biggest stores, bought a large quantity of foodstuffs for him to take back, stuffed some money into his shirt pocket, and got a youth of his aiga to drive him back to Malaelua in the pickup.

Chapter 13

They had succeeded in convincing Malaga that he was going to win the elections. Moaula was the only other candidate—'a decoy to stop anyone else from standing against you', Faleasa explained—and Malaga even paid Moaula's registration fee. Publicly all the matai had been instructed by Faleasa through Laaumatua and Moaula to vote for Malaga; anyone who voted for Moaula would show disloyalty to the council and would be banished after the elections. Secretly, however, a plan to effect Moaula's election had been initiated.

Early in the campaign some suspicious matai of Malaga's aiga warned him that Laaumatua and Moaula might be planning to unseat him, but one secret visit from Faleasa allayed Malaga's fears and he ordered all his aiga to trust Laaumatua and Moaula—anyone who didn't would be ostracised by their aiga.

It was almost impossible to keep anything as elaborate as an election plan a secret in Malaelua; some of the faithful would boast about it sooner or later. But Faleasa and Laaumatua used a very simple ploy. They knew that at least sixty per cent of the voters would support Laaumatua and Moaula, so all that the two council leaders need do was to meet each matai secretly, convince him of Malaga's evil, as it were, by revealing in lurid detail his scandalous past in New Zealand and his deportation, promise the voter financial rewards once Moaula was their MP, and subtly threaten him with banishment if he ever betrayed their secret bargain. On the other hand those matai who they thought would remain loyal to Malaga in all circumstances were sent for and encouraged to vote for him. In the end they calculated that they had seventy-five per cent of the vote. Faleasa, through Laaumatua, also instructed the pastor to preach sermons condemning hypocrisy, liquor, dishonesty, adultery, and using one's elected position to enrich oneself—all vices practised by Malaga, although his name was never mentioned.

About two weeks before election day a matai who knew the plan got drunk and bragged about Malaga's imminent destruction. Some of Malaga's relatives heard him and one of them rushed to Apia and told Malaga who rushed back to confront Faleasa who again emerged momentarily from his insanity, and in a short but ornately polite speech threatened to withdraw his support from Malaga if he continued to believe such vicious rumours. 'Would a blood relative betray another blood relative?' he asked Malaga. 'Would I have got you into parliament for nine long prosperous years if I hadn't trusted you, considered you the most able, most educated, most honest, most god-fearing man in Malaelua? Any more hints of suspicion on your part and I shall definitely withdraw my support.'

Malaga apologised profusely.

Election Day. An almost motionless mattress of cloud hid the morning sun and hung over Malaelua, holding the rising heat between it and the land. Everyone was sweating and would continue to do so until late that night when the cloud mattress would lift.

Sitting cross-legged outside his mosquito net—when most Malaeluans were still asleep—Faleasa gazed out at the placid lagoon through a gap between the dwellings across the road, sure that his plan would work and that by ten o'clock that night Malaga would have been destroyed. So, for the first time in almost a year, he decided to perform a short morning lotu: a lotu to whom wasn't important, only that the ritual would be a celebration of his victory.

As he sang the hymn he realised that Christianity had become unimportant to him; his rebellion and quest for freedom had reduced it to its rightful perspective as a social custom that one observed so as not to offend the majority of the people. His one regret was that he had never bothered to learn anything about the ancient religion of his people because the missionaries and his church had made him feel ashamed (and afraid) of it, had banished it into that historical realm which almost everyone now called 'The Time before the Coming of the Light' or 'The Days of Darkness and Paganism'. Even his father, who had been arrogantly proud of the faa-Samoa, had believed that the ancient religion was ludicrous, anathema, but a force to be wary of because it could, if encouraged, destroy a person's mind with a horrifying pagan darkness. How respectably human he had been, Faleasa accused himself. It had been easy to pursue the accepted ways and rituals, using them as crutches in his quest for status and power. In Malaeluan life the most heinous sin was to be a pagan or atheist so he had become an exemplary Christian; being an exemplary Christian and leader meant being a deacon so he had become a deacon. He had won the respect of village and church and had been appointed Malaelua's delegation leader to the annual LMS Church Fono at Malua. But he now realised that his whole existence as a Christian had meant nothing deeper than the necessity of being a Christian because it was expected of a good leader. He had clung to Christianity too in order to help dispel his fears of the meaninglessness of life: Christianity gave a meaning to the Void; but, he now reasoned, it was only one pattern of meaning; there were many others. It didn't matter now whether he was a Christian or not: he was soon to die and the Void didn't scare him any more—Pouliuli would embrace him, give him meaning.

Half way through the hymn some of his daughters and their children woke, sat up in their mosquito nets, and joined in the singing. Felefele was still asleep and snoring almost inaudibly. He picked up his ali and lobbed it at her net. It landed with a muffled thud on her shoulder and she was up and beginning to sing as if she hadn't been asleep at all.

For that day Faleasa had decided to regain his sanity publicly; this would further convince the voters to obey the instructions he had issued to them through the council leaders. Malaeluans were now used to his periods of sanity

—they usually coincided with the full moon, his grandchildren were fond of boasting to their friends.

The Malaelua polling booth, situated at the school in the middle of the village, was to open at ten o'clock; the other two villages, which made up the rest of the electorate, had a booth each. Faleasa's sons-in-law were to act as scrutineers at the Malaelua booth, and Laaumatua and Moaula and other loyal matai were to be responsible for the other booths. Before leaving for their booths Laaumatua and Moaula and many of their supporters joined Faleasa in his fale for a hearty meal of thick crunchy cabin bread, butter, jam, and cocoa which Malaga's aiga had provided. They laughed and joked throughout the meal but made no references to the secret plan. Some of the matai who had not been totally committed to the plan till that morning decided to commit themselves when they saw that Faleasa was sane again, interpreting his sanity as a holy omen of God's support for the plan.

After the others had left, Faleasa got his eldest son-in-law to cut his hair. Then he shaved and showered for the first time in weeks. Hidden behind a curtain which Felefele had strung across the fale he rubbed cocount oil into his skin, oiled his hair with a thick dollop of brilliantine and combed it until it shone, put on his most colourful shirt (the one with the red hibiscus flowers all over it which his children had given him for Christmas), hitched on a new chocolate-coloured lavalava which he had got Laaumatua to buy him the day before, wound his thick leather belt round his waist, and, while admiring his appearance in the full-length mirror beside the tallboy, decided that he looked a new man, a dignified stranger born out of the wrecked bundle of bone and sinew and wrinkles of the past months.

At that moment he heard a car approaching his fale. He peeped through the blinds and saw that it was Malaga in his pickup. He emerged quickly from behind the curtain and sat down cross-legged to await Malaga who, beaming a brilliant smile, came right up to him and shook his hand and kissed him on the cheek. Faleasa patted the mat next to him and Malaga sat down. Faleasa tried to ignore the strong smell of Malaga's perfume.

'You are well this morning?' Malaga asked.

Faleasa winked at him, 'Yes, I'm sane again and will remain so until your victory has been announced tonight.'

'Then what after that?' asked Malaga, handing him a large packet of American chewing gum, which Faleasa dropped into his shirt pocket.

'What do old men usually do after their last great victory?'

'Go on to other victories?' Malaga suggested.

'In Heaven or Hell?' said Faleasa, and they both laughed. Faleasa stopped laughing first and scrutinised Malaga's face closely. He suddenly wanted a confession from him, an admission of guilt, and then perhaps remorse and repentance. 'I am ready to die,' he said slowly. Malaga stopped laughing. 'But before I do so I must know the truth from you.' Malaga looked puzzled. 'There are bad stories being whispered about you.'

'What are these stories?' Malaga asked.

Gazing directly at Malaga as though he could see into his soul, Faleasa said, 'That you were deported from New Zealand...'

'A lie!' Malaga interrupted him. 'A malicious lie. Tell me who is responsible and I'll get him to admit to you that it's a lie!'

'...that in New Zealand you lived off a number of women and never attended that night school...'

'Lies, all lies!' Malaga insisted, and Faleasa noticed how his upper lip was now beaded with sweat like a series of transparent warts.

'...that you owe large debts to the principal Apia stores and that you are using your position to embezzle public funds...'

'Again lies, all malicious lies!'

'...and that you are leading a licentious and adulterous life....'

'Lies, all lies. I'd like to know who is spreading these lies about me!'

'You don't need to get worried. I believe you. That's all that matters, isn't it?' Faleasa reached over and patted

Malaga's trembling shoulder. Was there no honesty left in Malaga? He asked himself. No conscience? Had the disease infected him utterly? If Malaga was representative of the new leadership there was no hope for Malaelua or Samoa.

'Your unworthy son is grateful to his generous father who has placed so much faith and trust in him,' Malaga said.

'Yes,' Faleasa nodded, 'I have placed all my trust in you.' (So much so, he added to himself, that I feel no remorse whatsoever about destroying you.)

Before they drove to the polling booth Faleasa advised Malaga to cast his vote as soon as the booth opened and then to return immediately to Apia or else his aiga would find themselves having to give more money and food to the voters. 'Leave everything to me,' he said.

Malaga again expressed his heartfelt gratitude to his father and promised that, if he was made a cabinet minister, he would appoint Faleasa and Laaumatua to important government committees. He also took off his silver wrist watch—a present from a nephew he had sent to New Zealand, so he told Faleasa—and thrust it into Faleasa's hand. Faleasa tried to return it but Malaga insisted that he should keep it. 'It's only a very small gift for everything that you, Faleasa Osovae, my most precious father, have done and are doing for this most unworthy son.'

Nearly all the matai were assembled on the school veranda and under nearby trees waiting for the voting to start. Faleasa and Malaga went round greeting them.

Just before entering the booth to cast his vote Faleasa turned and addressed the matai. 'God has been kind and generous today in keeping away the rain and illnesses from us. As you can see, this decrepit old man is well again. God has been kind, so we must cast our votes for God and for the man God wants us to vote for. In the past few weeks God has addressed Himself to each and every one of us, telling us who He wants us to vote for. Today let us carry out our Almighty Father's wish. Let us pray:

'God, in Thy wisdom and justice, guide our hearts as we vote today. Show us the way so that our beloved district and country can find the path to Thee and away from the evil that some of our leaders are preaching and practising. Our district and country need Thee more than ever before. This Thy most worthless servant thanks Thee for restoring to him—at least for this most important day—the power of his weak mind so that he may cast his vote according to Thy will. . . . We ask all this in the name of Jesus Christ. Amen.'

That evening, a few hours before the final election results were to be broadcast over the national radio station, Faleasa summoned the heads of every loyal aiga to his fale. While they were enjoying a meal he advised them to prepare themselves in case Malaga's aiga reacted violently to the election results. They were to protect themselves but not to retaliate in kind, and if Malaga's aiga refused to listen to reason the council would banish it the next day. 'What about Malaga?' someone asked.

'Laaumatua and Moaula and I will deal with him,' Faleasa replied.

'Malaga will be too ashamed to show his face in Malaelua for quite a while,' said Laaumatua.

They laughed about that.

For a slow moment Faleasa couldn't believe he was awake; his eyes and ears were awake but his mind was still entangled in the dream. The shotgun fired again. The shrieking of women and children shattered the dream and he was fully awake and sitting up and gazing into the gloom, his heart beating wildly. Then, from the direction of the road, a blaring beam of light pierced through the fale blinds. Moaula and the other men and women pushed aside the blinds, and shielding their eyes with their hands gazed out into the blinding lights of a car. Faleasa knew it was Malaga but he wasn't afraid. By attacking his aiga Malaga was committing suicide: the council would now banish him and his aiga for sure.

Before Faleasa could stop him Moaula ripped down a row of blinds and stood up directly in the centre of the beam of light. With a shock of near panic Faleasa realised that he hadn't included Moaula's utter fearlessness in the equation; he must control his son or the violence would destroy them all. 'No!' he called to Moaula who was starting to move down the paepae towards the car. Moaula stopped.

Faleasa staggered to his feet and shuffled towards the gap in the blinds. 'Get the women and children out of here!' he ordered Felefele. When she refused to move he pulled her up, pushed her towards the children, and told her to take them out to their other fale. Felefele swallowed her sobbing and rushed to the children. As Faleasa picked his way over the paepae towards Moaula, who was standing defiantly still in the full anger of the light, he heard Malaga shouting: 'Madman! Madman! Madman, come out and taste my betrayal!'

Faleasa clutched Moaula's shoulder to restrain him from rushing headlong into the light and Malaga. He steadied his trembling legs, found solid footholds in the paepae, straightened up, hand still clutching Moaula's shoulder, and stared into the light. Shadows and outlines of men moved ominously behind it.

'Madman, you're going to regret what you've done to me!' Malaga called.

Moaula tried to shrug off Faleasa's hand but Faleasa gripped his shoulder more tightly. 'Go and see that our aiga are safe!' he whispered. Realising at that moment that his son would, without regret or reservation, die for him, Faleasa felt as if the beating of his own heart was that of his son's; he felt sure (and was happy in knowing it) that his choice of Moaula to replace him as head of their aiga and of Malaelua had been right. Moaula did not move. 'Go!' Faleasa repeated. Moaula moved backwards into the fale, and Faleasa heard him giving instructions to their aiga.

'What do you want?' Faleasa called towards the source of the light.

'You, madman!' was Malaga's reply.

'I may be mad but the victory is mine, isn't it?' No fear, only anger. In the past no one had dared threaten him. Now this beast, whose soul was infected beyond healing by the sickness, who didn't know what honour and integrity and courage and being a man were all about, this beast was daring to try to kill him! 'The victory is mine so who is the madman, you or me?' he called. The shotgun roared again and he shuddered momentarily. The row of blinds immediately to his right exploded into scattering fragments and smoke.

'You're forcing me to kill you!' Malaga called.

'That's what you came here to do, so do it. Or have you lost the courage already?'

In the short hush that followed, Faleasa heard Malaga talking to his men. Then he saw two of them—more darkness than men—step into the beam of light and advance slowly towards him, as though the light was pushing them forward and making them appear as if they were on fire. Events were moving beyond his control and others would suffer if he couldn't regain control immediately. 'Stop your dogs!' he called to Malaga. 'This affair is between you and me. Our aiga must not suffer!'

The men stopped.

'Madman, you excreted on the honour and good name of my aiga in what you did today!' Malaga said, and called to his men, 'Go ahead!'

Just as the two men reached the bottom of the paepae Faleasa glimpsed a shadow rushing out from the darkness on his right. It was Moaula. Clutched in his right hand was a bushknife. Faleasa gasped with a desperate fear. The circle had tilted beyond his control. The accusing figure of the insane old man who could not complete his circle because he, Faleasa, had deliberately thrown away the centre stunned his mind. Desperately he stepped forward to try to stop his son who, except for Laaumatua, was the only person he had ever genuinely and deeply loved. 'No! No!' he called to Moaula. He tripped and fell forward. The rocks of the paepae rushed up to shock him with a ringing pain. He tried to push himself up. In that instant before he lost consciousness he saw the flashing bushknife whipping down and a man screaming, screaming, his arms outstretched towards the sky's black dome, his head thrown back, his mouth wide open and screaming soundlessly and forever.

And he knew he would not be forgiven. Not ever.

When Malaga saw one of his men, a cousin, being killed, he dropped his shotgun and started to scramble into his pickup to flee. But Moaula caught him and killed him with one swift unforgiving slash of the bushknife.

For the two killings Moaula was sentenced to life imprisonment.

Malaga's aiga was banished by the council.

Elefane and his wife Povave and their large brood returned to Malaelua the day they received the news of Moaula's sentence. The Aiga Faleasa, controlled by Felefele, conferred the Faleasa title on Elefane. In the by-election to find a successor for Moaula in parliament Elefane was elected unopposed.

Chapter 14

Laaumatua grabbed his walking stick and hurried towards the church.

On the way he remembered how he and Faleasa as boys had seen that strange old man sitting on the church steps and had helped to take him to Faleasa's home. It was nearly noon, and shadows were nesting thirstily in the roots of the trees and the fale and other buildings like on that day they had found the old man. Laaumatua tried to dismiss the memory but it persisted.

From across the empty malae he could see a group of children in front of the church. They were jeering at Faleasa who was standing on the topmost step, with his arms outstretched to the dazzling sky, his mouth fixed in a soundless scream, his long hair and beard as brilliantly white as the whitewashed church walls. And for Laaumatua the memory of that other old man and the sight of Faleasa on the steps became indistinguishably one—one lucid memory giving meaning to what his friend had become.

He chased the children away and hobbled up the steps towards his friend, his walking stick thudding into the concrete. Faleasa looked as though he had emerged out of the fabric of the church itself and no one would ever shift him from those steps.

From a few paces away Laaumatua smelt his friend's unwashed stench. He reached out to him, but Faleasa dropped his arms to his sides, turned his fixed gaze on him, and edged away. Tears filled Laaumatua's eyes. Faleasa continued to stare at him as he reached out and held his right arm and whispered, 'Faleasa, let's go to my home.' Faleasa shook his head. 'My home is your home,' Laaumatua said, with tears running down his face. Unable to bear Faleasa's vulnerable eyes, he looked away, and for a few minutes they remained motionless.

Then unexpectedly Laaumatua felt Faleasa's warm hand on his back; he turned, to see his friend smiling sadly at him. He wound his arm round Faleasa's waist and helped him down the steps and across the parched malae in the shadowless noon to his home where the women of his aiga washed Faleasa and cleaned and bandaged his sores and fed him.

While Faleasa slept that afternoon, Laaumatua sat beside him.

It's all vanity, isn't it? You wanted to be free in the last years of your life but that too was vanity. Look at you now, my friend. Just gristle and suffering and weeping sores. We lost out a long time ago, my beloved friend. The new world is for creatures like Malaga and Elefane; they're everywhere because they're of the times. . . . Sleep on, my most precious friend, safe in the embrace of Pouliuli, the Great Darkness out of which we came and to which we must all return. Sleep on. . . . You have escaped while I must continue to live with my crippled self and protect you, as I have done without your knowing—you see I still can't destroy my vanity—nearly all our life together. Me, without Mua, my wife, and Mose, the son I possessed and then betrayed by trying to turn him into someone he did not want to be—the only other creatures I ever allowed myself to love in all my pain and worthlessness and vanity.

Sleep on, my friend, while the world dreams of terror. . . .

Glossary

aiga   family, extended family
aitu   ghost, evil spirit
ali   wooden headrest
alii   matai with an alii title
alofa   love, compassion; a present, a gift
aualuma   group of untitled women in a village
cacao   (Spanish) cocoa-producing tree
faa-Samoa   Samoan way of doing things, Samoan way of life
faalifu talo   taro cooked with coconut cream
faamafu   home-brewed beer
fale   Samoan house
faleoloa   store
fautasi   long boat rowed by oarsmen
fofo   healer
fono   council, legislative assembly
gogo   tern
ietoga   fine mat
kāupoe   cowboy
kava   ceremonial drink made from roots of kava plant
lafo   presentation of money
lapiti   rabbit
lavalava   skirt-like, wrap-around garment
lotu   church service, prayers
luau   young taro leaves cooked with coconut cream
malae   meeting area (Maori, marae)
mango   (Portuguese) Indian tree with flashy yellowish-red fruit
matai   titled head of an aiga
Meauli   Negro
momoli   gift of food and money given by a leader to his

village or district when he visits them

ola   large basket, usually made of bamboo

paepae   stone foundation of a fale

palagi or papalagi   person of European stock

palusami   *see* luau

penisini   benzine

pisupo   tinned corned beef

pouliuli   darkness

pulu   Samoan tree

saofai   ceremony at which matai titles are bestowed

sea   edible sea slug

seevae   shoes

siva   to dance (v.), a Samoan dance (n.)

suipi   card game

tapa cloth   cloth made from bark of mulberry plant (not a Samoan word)

taro   (Samoan, talo) edible bulbous root

taulealea   untitled man or men (pl. taulelea)

tautoga   oath-taking ceremony

tooñai   Sunday lunch

tulafale   matai who holds an orator's title

tuua   senior orator in a village: usually owes appointment to his knowledge of history, genealogy, and protocol and to his wisdom

umu   oven made of stones

yam   edible tuberous root